S0-ARM-744

Crime Scenes

stories

Spineless Wonders
PO Box 220
Strawberry Hills
New South Wales, Australia, 2012
https://shortaustralianstories.com.au

First published by Spineless Wonders 2016

Editorial assistance & copyediting by Bronwyn Mehan, Annie Parkinson, Maximilian Korbas and Emma Walsh.

Typeset in Adobe Garamond Pro

Printed and bound by Ingram Spark Australia

National Library of Australia Cataloguing-in-Publication entry
Edited by Zane Lovitt
Crime Scenes An anthology of short stories
1st ed.
978 1 9250 52237(pbk.)
A823.4

ISBN 978 1 9250 52237 (pbk)
ISBN 978 1 9250 52251 (ebk)

Crime Scenes
stories

Edited by

Zane Lovitt

spineless wonders

www.shortaustralianstories.com.au

Contents

Introduction

Long ago I heard it said that crime fiction is the king of genres. Even to a writer of crime fiction, it seemed a lofty claim. My instinct was to straddle my high horse and pontificate on the subjective nature of art, to declare that one person's Picasso is another's arse-pick-o, to deem the truth unknowable in the Hegelian, objective sense.

That response is technically correct and painfully boring.

Long ago I heard it said that the only rule of writing fiction is, Don't Be Boring.

So allow me to offer three reasons why crime fiction is the metaphorical king of the literary jungle.

First, it sells. People read it. Nuff said.

Second, nothing gets you turning the page like suspense. It's the reason we experience stories – to be made to want to know what happens next. Laughing, crying, learning; these can be a lovely bonus, an end in themselves, but our addiction to stories is our addiction to that sense of fever and urgency when we forget where we are, forget who we are. When we flip off the pilates class planned for six tomorrow morning because we can't put the cursed book down and turn off the light – otherwise known as suspense.

Yes, you find it across all genres. Science fiction can make you hanker to find out how the robot stole the virus from the spaceship. Romance novels ask you to wait, chapter upon chapter, before telling you if the squash champion and the neurosurgeon live happily ever after. And you almost skip forward, desperate, guilty, just to ease that glorious ball of tension in your stomach.

But here's the thing: the crime section of the bookshop is the one place where you know the writer set out to do that. For all other writing, it's what happens when the author knows their craft. For crime fiction, it's the atomic purpose. It's why the work exists: to make the reader turn the page with fumbling, sweaty fingers.

Third, crime fiction is the closest we have to a genre that directly reflects our ordinary lives. The challenges faced by characters in crime fiction are the same that you and I encounter every day, but for these characters the stakes are so much higher: a suitcase full of money, a prison sentence, a grievous assault, or (most often) life itself. But beneath this contrivance, the characters' dilemmas are our dilemmas.

I may argue with my brother and we may take our turns feeling humiliated, or offended, or neglected, but what's at stake for us is fairy floss compared to what's at stake for Michael and Fredo Corleone in *The Godfather*. And because the stakes are high, that conflict *has* to be resolved.

Crime fiction is a Trojan horse, sneaking in relevant, even important information for our lives under the guise of escapism. Yes, this too is a feature of all genre-writing, but crime fiction is where the characters are the most ordinary, the most recognisable, the most us.

This hot little book you hold in your hands is filled with more examples. 'Saying Goodbye' is, on the surface, the final thoughts of a crooked cop and his ignominious end. Underneath, it depicts the lasting shame so many adult children feel for their fathers. In 'Death Star', a revenge plot blossoms in rural Australia, pulling back the curtain on the lack of meaning and opportunity for small-town youth.

You're sceptical, I know. Perhaps you loathe crime fiction, consider its conventions clichés and its conflict dull. Perhaps you only picked up this book because you know someone who reads crime, their birthday is approaching and you want to be sure this font meets with your exacting standards. Well, don't buy it for someone else. Buy it for you. There's a special treat for your kind at the end.

More likely, you're loving how prejudiced you think I am. You're superior like a marriage counsellor: cri-fi isn't better or worse, just different. You are a student of the world, a diner at the banquet of literature where no course is served nonpareil.

And I get that. We are not so different, you and I.

But I invite you to dismount that horse, to unclench and find within these pages that heady pulse you felt as a child walking the library aisles, when books smelled of musty excitement and the musty librarian needn't have bothered to shush anyone because the book you'd drawn from the shelf was authentic, faithful to the first principles of storytelling:

Make the reader turn the page.

Make them forget where they are.

Who they are.

Don't be boring.

Fuck pilates.

Nuff said.

Zane Lovitt, 2016

CRIME SCENES

The Turn

Amanda O'Callaghan

It's the turn that tells you. There you are, idly taking in a man carrying a black bin bag, making his way down a lane. You know the bag's heavy – you see that – and you've got nothing better to do than just sit in the car and think that maybe he works in one of those restaurants, so the bag's full of slops, pulpy and unstable, a horror show if it splits open. You think maybe he's just been cleaning out rubbish, sorting out his spare room or his study. He might live in those apartments stacked above the shops. But you decide that he doesn't look like the studying kind. Funny how you know these things based on nothing, from just a glance. He's got his back to you, so you can't see his face; no idea about hair or skin colour. He's wearing dark clothes and some sort of beanie on his head, but that's all you could say. Has he got an unusual walk? Maybe you're imagining it. He's not moving very fast with the weight of the bag, so he might be middle-aged, or older. You know he's not well, the way he carries his shoulders a fraction too high. Emphysema. Might be lung cancer. A sick, old man taking out his rubbish. All these things go through your mind in a matter of seconds.

'What are you thinking about?' Jackie used to ask me all the time.

'Nothing,' I'd tell her. But truth is, you're always thinking of something, always noticing.

The guy's almost at the back of the lane now. The traffic's heavy enough. Not much business around. He's about to disappear, and you've lost interest. But then he turns. Still holding the bag clear of the ground, he stops, swivels his body round towards you. You see a flash of white-skinned neck. He looks straight at you, like he can see you, only he can't because you're sitting in the dark, waiting for the lights to change. But it's the turn that makes you look more closely. It's not like he'd heard something scrabbling near the bins, or footsteps behind him. This is slow, deliberate. He turns because he's checking no-one's watching.

But you are.

*

'You're a gloomy sod, Robbie Quinn', Jackie used to say.

She always called me by my full name. Coming from her, it never felt strange. Same with the way she called me a sod. There was no malice in it. She said it about a lot of people. 'A poor old sod was brought in this morning and you should have seen his leg…' Jackie's sod was harmless, affectionate even, unless she told you to sod off. Then you'd know she was annoyed. She sounded most English when she said that – the little snap of her accent coming through. It used to make me smile.

And, no, I wasn't gloomy. Not back then. Jackie always thought that having a quiet moment meant you were getting depressed. She didn't like to think about things too deeply. Some days all I wanted to do was just sit at the table, sip my coffee and stare out into the street for half an hour. But it bothered Jackie. She'd start shuffling papers, pushing in chairs. 'When's your shift start?' she'd say. 'Aren't you going to your mother's first? That coffee'll be cold as charity by now.' She'd annoy me out of my thoughts and I'd get going again, saving my quiet time for when she was at the hospital. I sit at the window a lot now. Everything stays where I leave it. The coffee goes as cold as charity, whatever that means. When I turn to look into the street, I notice everything.

*

A crowd is a terrible thing. I know it's foolish to say so because mostly a crowd has a purpose: commuters, shoppers, hospital visitors – the posse of media in my front yard. In a crowd, pretty well everyone has a place to be. But for me, even after all this time, it's different, unnerving. I look at every face, assessing every shape and size. I get entangled in the impossible knot of all those lives: the way they walk, hold their heads, their voices as they pass. Once, near the old bus station, I could hear a frantic call, 'Robbie, Robbie', and the accent was English and I said to myself, *Don't turn around. She always said your full name. It's not her. It can't be her.* But at the last minute, I did turn, and I saw a woman with her arms outstretched, and a black dog racing away trailing a glittery red lead. And when someone caught the leash as the dog shot past, bringing him up tight like a cartoon character, front paws pedalling the air, I burst into a crazy cackle. Too loud, too high. And everyone turned – some with frozen smiles from watching the dog – and they all stared because I was a man laughing alone in a crowd. A man with no place to go.

*

THE TURN

They thought it was me in the beginning. Some of the papers, all of the cops. Can't say I blame them. *Routine procedure*, I heard that a lot. Mostly, it was two cops. One almost small enough to be a jockey, except he had huge hands. The other about my size, normal enough, but with something of the cowboy about him. He had a Clint Eastwood squint in one eye when he spoke, like he was looking into a mirage down a long highway. If he'd been an accountant or a bus driver you wouldn't even notice it. But a detective – it was almost comical. Once, after he'd been questioning me for a long time, I could see the squint forming, and I felt myself starting to smile.

'Something funny, Mr Quinn?' he said, and that eye would shrink even more. The jockey never said much, just watched, hunched over the table, those hands all knotted up in front of him. Once, late, when Clint had his face up close and I was feeling light-headed, I just burst out laughing. The sound bounced all over the room. An older guy in uniform looked in at the door for a few seconds, went away without a word.

'Your wife is missing, Mr Quinn,' Clint said, 'and you're laughing. Can you explain that?'

And he looked over at the jockey, who just shook his head and re-knotted his hands.

*

If Jackie had been there she could have told them that I always laugh when things are really bad. That I laughed at my own sister's funeral. Poor Lisa. 'You're a stupid sod, Robbie Quinn,' Jackie had whispered under her breath, passing me a huge folded handkerchief. And I'd sobbed and tittered into the green tartan and everyone except Jackie moved a little bit away, so that when my poor sister was safely out of sight I found myself almost alone, as if I'd been at someone else's graveside, a different funeral. The smell of the fresh-turned earth that day was oddly pleasant. When the vicar turned back and said, 'Can I help you, Mr Quinn?' I let Jackie answer for me.

'I'm taking him home now,' she said, and she slipped her hand under my arm and turned me towards the road. Tender. Sometimes things could be really tender between us. We actually walked home that day, though it was miles. Halfway there, where the road bends away from the edge of town like it's trying to escape all the dullness, I threw the handkerchief into the Torrens. For once, Jackie didn't say a word, just did up her top button where a sharpish breeze was pushing in. When I turned back to the water, the handkerchief was floating away like a small, checked raft.

*

Four miles. That's the distance between here and the hospital. Yes, I know it's supposed to be kilometres but Jackie never broke the habit of talking in miles, so I kept it too. I never walked to my shift, not once, but Jackie liked walking. 'I hate those smelly buses,' she'd say. We didn't use the car for work. 'Rotten sods, ripping us off with the parking.'

I wouldn't let her walk at night, and she'd moan about that sometimes, tell me about the freaks on the bus. But she'd humour me. 'Take a taxi if you miss the last bus,' I'd tell her. 'Yeah, yeah, moneybags,' she'd say. There's only two street cameras between the hospital and our house. One points at the footpath, one at the road. You learn this stuff. Jackie was picked up on both of them, walking quickly. On the second one, she stops and unbuttons her jacket because she's got too warm. She was hurrying because she was late leaving the hospital and it's dark, except for the light from Roy's Discount Meats spilling into the road.

They showed me the camera footage of Jackie a couple of times. I could hear Clint breathing beside me as I watched, feel his eyes on the side of my face. As Jackie walks out of view – the last sight of her – her coat, which is slung over one shoulder, lifts in the wind like a purple cape. She looks back, as if someone has called her. Then she turns towards home, stepping into a great pool of darkness.

*

Truth is, I was thinking about leaving her. There was never any big fight, no major issue. Most of the time, to use Jackie's words, we mucked along pretty well. I just wanted to find a bit of peace on my own. I like my own company, always have. The night shifts used to kill some of the others, but not me. I liked the hush that came over everything up in the ward late at night. It's always had a magical quality; anything felt possible. But maybe, on the quiet nights, there was too much time to think. And sometimes, I admit it, I thought about a life without Jackie. My feeble half-notions about leaving her make me cringe now. It all seems so petty, after everything that followed.

*

'I thought you were starting early today,' I said to Jackie as she sat down at the breakfast table on our last day together.

'Phoned in sick,' she said. Her voice was tight. She hadn't brushed her hair, which was unusual. She was hugging her coffee cup with two hands, holding it so hard that I thought it might crack open and slosh over us both. I ate my toast and watched her, the crunching loud in my ears. Jackie knew about Ida Costello in Bed 6. I could see that. She was never off that damn phone of hers.

'You know I can't stay,' she said, staring. 'You know I can't get up every day and look at you, knowing what went on.'

I was surprised at how angry she was. 'Christ, Jackie, she was nearly ninety. The woman had one lung. She was in a lot of—'

'Don't say it!' Jackie actually shrieked those words. Later, our neighbour would tell Clint he heard it, clear as a bell. We weren't shouters, generally. Jackie was up on her feet then. She walked over to the window and stood there for a long time, her back to me. Then she turned and said, very quietly, 'You don't get to choose these things, Robbie Quinn. Nobody gets to choose. You decided about Lisa, didn't you?'

She could see by my face it was true.

'Your own sister, for god's sake.' Jackie looked very small, standing there in her dressing-gown, her balled fists like little apples in the pale pink pockets. 'And poor old Ida.'

I started to move towards her but Jackie looked like she might jump through the window if I came any closer. 'It was you at Welgrove General, wasn't it?' Jackie said. I was close enough to see her eyes fill with tears. 'That big woman with the sarcoma, she was the first, wasn't she? And then poor old Mrs Lacey.'

'Jackie,' I said, but more words wouldn't come. She was looking at me with repulsion. 'You covered it up well,' she said, her voice suddenly nurse-calm. Evelyn Lacey's face loomed at me out of the past. Relieved. That's how she'd looked. There was a bit of talk after she died – that nosy new registrar – but nothing came of it and we both left Welgrove soon afterwards.

Now, looking at Jackie's disgusted face, I didn't know whether to feel angry or sad. I thought she'd realised about Lisa. 'It's for the best,' Jackie said at the time, when my sister was finally gone. The best. But now I could see the truth: Jackie's words weren't some coded message of approval. *For the best* was just another cliché. Hospitals are full of them. Doctors, nurses, counsellors – even the tea lady never shuts up. It's what we say when we can't make things better. Jackie had never mentioned the deaths at Welgrove until Ida Costello died. Not in any specific sense. Any blaming sense. But something must have clicked for her with Ida's death. Everything seemed obvious after that.

'How could you?' she'd said, suddenly breaking down, fleeing towards the bedroom. I knew then she'd leave. In the doorway, only half turning as if she could no longer bear to look at me, she said, 'It's murder, you stupid fucking sod.'

*

I wasn't sorry about Ida Costello. 'Say a prayer for me, won't you?' Ida used to say, most days. I told her I wasn't religious, every time, but she'd just say, 'Well, maybe today.' She wasn't hoping to get better; she knew enough to know that wouldn't happen. She was hoping she'd die. That's what all these hypocrites can't accept, what Jackie could never accept: these people had had enough. My poor cancer-raddled sister wanted to die. 'Help me, Robbie,' she said, and I knew exactly what she meant. But helping Lisa didn't come easily. It's much more straightforward when they're just patients.

Welgrove General is a big country hospital: wide wooden verandahs at the front, farmland in one direction, bush in the other, wallabies on the back lawn of an evening. Beautiful place. I met Jackie there. We stayed six years before we moved to Adelaide. But Welgrove General's like every other hospital: people get sick, people get better, people die. Jackie was wrong about one thing, though. Yes, there was that woman with the rhabdomyosarcoma – Judy was her name – and poor old Evelyn Lacey with everything under the sun. But Frank Easton was the first. He was a retired barley farmer, huge guy, never smoked a day in his life, sang in the local choir. Bone cancer – primary – then it raced through his body. But he was the man who would not die.

One night, late, Frank rang the call button. The pain must have been bad. He asked me, straight out, to finish him off. You'd be surprised how common that is. I gave him the usual blather – told him it was impossible, strict protocols, rules, laws. He looked straight at me, as much as he could; he'd lost control of one of his eyes by then. He grabbed my wrist, still a surprisingly strong grasp. The rain was hitting off the roof so hard I could barely hear him.

'Find a way,' he said.

So I did. Odd how I didn't give it much thought at the time. It felt like a job to be done, just like all the other jobs. Drugs, of course. What else? There's not a thing I don't know about them. The doctors think the nurses haven't got a clue but, honestly, it's usually the other way around. It's a point of pride for me: three generations of pharmacists and a couple of secret addicts thrown in for good measure. I knew what I was doing.

'All the best, Frank,' I said to him.

THE TURN

I felt faintly nervous when it was over. But there was no trouble. Poor old Frank was out of his pain. No-one suspected a thing. Not even Jackie.

But Frank had a son, a surly little bastard called Frank Junior who'd come up to the hospital most days to make sure all his father's finances were sorted in his favour. Day after day he'd sit by the bed, buttoning down every last corner of the farm and all the rest. In a weak moment, old Frank was fool enough to tell him that he was thinking of approaching one of the nurses on the late shift to help finish him off. I think I actually walked in on them having this conversation.

'Don't be stupid, Dad,' Frank Junior told him, as I came towards them. 'You've got the solicitor coming in tomorrow. The house thing.' Old Frank hushed him with a waving hand, and Junior sat glowering at me from beside the bed, saying no more. Of course, I had no idea what they were talking about at the time.

But it turns out old Frank didn't want Junior – who must have been fifty, at least – to get the family home. He was going to inherit pretty well everything else, but the house was going to Frank's niece, not his son. She came in, near the end, and left in tears. Real tears. Frank had made his decision; he was ready to go.

The following morning, as I was packing up the room – old Frank's body had been moved downstairs by then – Junior came in behind me, closed the door.

'Think you're pretty clever, don't you?' he said, standing very close. I could smell his toothpaste. He was a severe asthmatic; I could hear the pull in his chest as he waited for my response.

The barley farm was going to kill him, I thought, with some satisfaction. I didn't turn around, just kept packing up the kit.

'I know it was you,' he said. His father was barely cold and it was pretty obvious that he'd already had word that he didn't get the house in town. 'I'm going to make you sorry, Nurse Quinn,' he said.

Junior was smart enough to know that he could never prove anything, medically. He had taken a long, hard look at me from his perch in the corner of his father's room and rightly guessed I'd have it all covered. But I remember thinking, as his eyes followed me around the room each day, that he might be a man who could make real trouble. In a hospital, you get pretty good at analysing people. You see everything across those beds. Frank Junior was a hater, I saw that – a vindictive little hater. And I let that slide. I only made one mistake but it was a big one: I put Frank Junior out of my mind.

*

'Do you remember a guy called Easton. From Welgrove?' Jackie said, one night, warming up her curry after her shift. I felt my heart race almost instantly. 'Easton? No.'

'Yes, you do', she said. 'The barley farmer. Frank Easton. He was in Malloy Ward. The one who used to sing sometimes. Hung on for ages, poor sod.'

'Oh, yeah. What about him?'

'Remember he had a son?' Jackie said. 'Wiry little guy, about fifty. Not very nice. Came in all the time.'

'Vaguely,' I lied.

'Saw him this evening.' Jackie was banging sticky rice off the spoon on the side of the saucepan, making an incredible racket. I'd already eaten. I was sipping a beer, watching her from across the table. 'He was called Frank as well,' she said. 'Remember? Frank Junior.'

'Junior' I said, keeping my voice flat.

'Yeah. He was on the bus,' she said, crashing her cutlery onto the table. Was there ever a moment, I wondered, when Jackie was doing something quietly?

I took another sip. 'It wouldn't have been him. Didn't he inherit the old man's farm? That's a day's drive away. What would he be doing in the middle of Adelaide?'

'Would have made a pretty puny farmer if you ask me,' she said, forking in the curry. 'Bet he sold it, or went bust. Anyway, it was definitely him. Don't you remember he had a tattoo on his hand? Um…' She held up her hands to work out where she'd seen it on him. 'On his left hand. A little thistle, a red-and-green thistle down near his thumb. You must have noticed it. It was definitely him.'

'Where did he get off?' I said, remembering that tattooed hand lying flat on his father's bed. I turned my beer bottle in its pool of condensation. Jackie had pulled the newspaper towards her and wasn't listening. 'Jackie!'

She jumped. 'Jesus, what's wrong with you? I don't know where. Oh, yes I do, it was the same stop as me. After I got off. He didn't see me though. He was reading something on the bus. I only saw the tattoo at the last minute.'

The beer suddenly seemed too cold, sending a shiver to my brain. 'Did he walk the same way as you?'

She looked up from the paper. 'Hmm? No. He didn't walk anywhere. He sat down at the bus-stop and was looking for something in a bag. I saw him when I crossed the road.' She went back to the stove. Turning to me, serving spoon in hand, she said, 'Want some more curry?'

*

I always thought he'd come after me. I can honestly say I never once thought about Jackie. What does that tell you? Maybe a man in love would have thought of her straight away, tried to protect her from bad people. But I wasn't that man.

Jackie's been listed as missing for six years now. A cold case, they call it. Clint retired to a walnut farm – squinting at aphids these days, I guess. Most of the media pack lost interest pretty quickly. There were richer pickings to be had. There was one journalist who used to turn up on my doorstep every year around the time Jackie first disappeared. The last time I saw him I surprised myself by asking him in, making him coffee. He got chatty, told me he wrote about the economy, mostly, but he was keen to get into investigative work, write a book. He told me he was examining Jackie's case as a kind of hobby. A hobby. I knew I had to pack up when I heard that, leave Adelaide for good. I was starting to feel rage rather than pity, and that's not a logical reason to kill someone. Well, not just anyone.

*

Melbourne's the kind of city to get lost in, only I know pretty well every street these days. I drive a taxi. Seriously. No more hospitals for me. Taxi driving's harder than it looks: long hours and some pretty despicable people, drunk and sober. Nice ones too, of course, and some days, if I'm in the mood and they mention some affliction or other, I give them a free consultation. There's always a good tip at the end of that ride.

There's a coffee shop near the big tyre place on Roberts Road. I used to go regularly, mostly because none of the other drivers stop there. It was winter, I remember; everyone had coats on. I'd bent my head to take a careful sip of coffee – they always serve it scalding hot – and I heard a voice I knew behind me. 'Ham and *cheese*, not ham and tomato.' A man, pissed off, complaining about his toasted sandwich. The girl behind the counter apologised, gave him his money back when he wouldn't wait for a replacement. I didn't turn my head, just hunkered down inside my collar, kept the coffee mug close to my face. Had he seen me? All I saw was the back of a man in a longish navy coat and a dark red beanie. A woman with a twin pram carved up any further view of him as he left, but, standing up, I could see him at the corner. He didn't look back. I watched as he pulled one of his gloves off with his teeth to sort out his money. Even from that distance, I could see the dark blob of tattoo near his wrist as he turned towards the train and disappeared.

I knew there was a chance Frank Junior could be in Melbourne. I'd met old Frank's niece – the one who got the house – when I went back to the area for my mother's funeral. She came to the service. 'Thank you for being so good to Uncle Frank,' she said, pressing my hand in the overheated chapel.

'He was a way better man than I'll ever be,' I said. That was true. Later, she told me the barley farm was gone: 'Junior sold it for half nothing. Said he hated the country. Said farming was for idiots.'

I thought it would be easy, but I didn't see Frank Junior again for a long time. I drove. I had good days and bad days. I waited. I dreamed – literally dreamed – of him getting into my cab without realising it was me at the wheel. I had special locks fitted, just in case.

*

It took me almost a full day before I finally twigged about the man I'd seen in the lane. I was at home, drinking coffee, staring out the window. Scenes from the previous few days were looping through my mind: that nice big tip from old Ingrid; the Scottish guy with one arm; the truck roll-over on Hodda Terrace – all the jumble and flare of ordinary life. And then, half watching someone in the street lugging a heavy bag, I realised what I'd seen the night before: the man with the rubbish bag, the way he walked, the way he turned. The thought stunned me. At last. The man was Frank Junior.

It was a Thursday night. Late-night shopping – busy for me, most times. I was thinking about Jackie, if you can believe that. I'd gone a fair while without giving her too much thought, then for a week or so she kept coming into my mind. Robbie Quinn. Robbie Quinn. There she was, pecking away at me, just like before. His flat was above the noodle shop. I almost laughed out loud when I pulled the corner of a letter out of his mailbox and I saw his new name: just one letter stuck on the front of his old name. Frank

THE TURN

Neaston. Pathetic. At least I had the decency to change mine completely.

*

Frank Junior always took his rubbish out last thing at night. It's never a good idea to be predictable. His death didn't get any more coverage than it deserved. *A body discovered … a laneway off Drummond Street … the schoolboys are receiving counselling … not believed to be suspicious.* So said the woman on the news. The next night she announced that the body had been identified as Frank Neaston, retired labourer. I actually chortled. Frank Junior never laboured for anything in his life, except maybe that last breath. I used ketamine, mostly. Not ideal, but my options are limited these days. Hypodermic, of course. It was late; I knew he'd be dead by the time he was found.

The TV showed a long shot of the laneway. The woman from the noodle bar was leaving a small bunch of flowers. Uncannily, she got the spot exactly right: just left of the big wheelie bin. 'He came in on Tuesday nights,' she said to the camera, standing awkwardly close. 'Beef noodles.'

The camera panned across a small crowd of bystanders staring down the now-empty lane. A couple of kids chewing gum, a very tall man, a few women. The reporter, a young guy with a square thatch of red hair, signed off, 'Back to you, Elena.'

And then it was over. I'd been watching all this, mulling over the mixed feelings I was having: relief, pleasure, that odd flatness. I was half thinking that I might move back to Adelaide, now that everything was settled. There was no more danger now. No prospect of exposure. The vacant faces of the crowd in the laneway had just faded into the next piece of news. Suddenly, I was on my feet. One of the women in that crowd, that one with the white jumper. It couldn't be her. But the way she turned her head, her chin in profile, her hands balled in her pockets. It was Jackie.

*

Every day I tell myself it was not her. A look-alike, that's all. *Jackie's dead, and you know it.* I say that over and over. I work hard at keeping everything tamped down. *You know it better than anyone else. For certain.* I force her out of my mind. The look on her face. Her voice. I think of nothing, just sit at the window, watch the world go by. After Frank Junior – after Jackie – I thought I'd feel … free. I thought the past could be filed away and forgotten. At peace. That's all I've ever wanted. A bit of peace. But when I empty my head, that's when I hear it. *Robbie Quinn. Robbie Quinn.* In a crowd, especially, I hear that voice. And when I wheel around, my eyes raking through all the bodies, I swear I catch a glimpse of her face, turning away.

Three-Pan Creek Gift

Peter Corris

A CLIFF HARDY STORY

I was reading a history of professional foot running in Australia. It had a chapter on the Three-Pan Creek Gift near Willow Bend in the southern tablelands, which, for over a hundred years, had been the next richest professional footrace to Victoria's Stawell Gift. It was still big in the 70s but faded as interest in the sport waned. It died in the early 80s to be revived in 1988 when Willow Bend got some Federal funding to put it on for one last time as a Bicentennial event. The race attracted sponsors.

Reading about it reminded me of my involvement with Travis Cooke. I had a behind-the-scenes story the writer of the book didn't know about. The Gift originated in the years after gold was discovered, very late in the piece in the 1870s. In the early alluvial phase a legend was born that you could make a substantial strike after panning a particular creek just three times. Hence the name of the creek and the establishment of the race in a paddock near Willow Bend and its eventual adoption as part of the annual Willow Bend Agricultural Show.

Held in early October before the weather got too hot, the show drew people from all over the district and further afield – the south coast and Canberra, once the capital started to grow after World

War II. The stakes were high while gold was being found, with miners stripping down to their underwear to make the hundred-yard dash in bare feet. A number of Aboriginals won the race.

Over the years the winner's prize stayed attractive as young athletes – boxers, footballers, swimmers, axemen and shearers – tried to make some extra money during the Depression and later. The bookies naturally took an interest and betting became a big feature of the race. For the Bicentennial event the competition among sprinters and bookmakers was intense. The prize money was $25 000 and an officially sanctioned handicapping system was in place.

I was surprised when I got a phone call from professional sprinter Travis Cooke in September of 1988. I'd heard of him because he'd finished second twice in the Stawell Gift and had won some other big races. I had more than a passing interest in professional running. An uncle had won the Stawell Gift in the 1940s and was a family hero. I was a useful sprinter in my younger days but better over 200 metres than 100 and that, then and now, wasn't a glamour event. I hadn't quite inherited my uncle's speed out of the blocks or over the distance and regretted it.

I agreed to meet Travis Cooke where he was training on a grass track marked out for him on an oval in the grounds of Sydney University where he worked as a fitness coach and gym instructor for several of the university's sports teams.

Late on a cold afternoon, I stood near the cricket nets while Cooke did 20-metre spurts, running forwards, then backwards, then skipping sideways. In earlier times, sprinters tended to be middle-sized or compact men – Jesse Owens, Mike Agostini, Hec

Hogan, my uncle Clem. Later, wherever they came from, they were mostly big – Alberto Juantorena, Darren Clark, Carl Lewis. Travis was six-foot-four in the old money, and probably weighed 78 kilos plus. Despite that, in motion, he appeared to be as airborne and graceful as a ballet dancer.

I watched him go through these demanding exercises for twenty minutes. When he stopped and came over to me he was sweating freely but wasn't significantly out of breath.

'Cliff Hardy,' I said.

'Travis.'

We shook hands. Strong grip, hand calloused from working weights and exercise machines.

'I'd put money on you in anything involving running backwards or sideways.'

'Are you taking the piss?'

'Sorry, it's a bad habit. I wasn't that keen on meeting here. It's cold and I knew you could run.'

'Yeah, well I just wanted to show you I was in serious training.'

'I'm convinced. For what?'

He towelled off. 'The Three-Pan Creek Gift. You've heard of it?'

'I have. My uncle Clem ran in it as a back marker. Didn't win.'

'Well then, you'll know that it's on again for one last time. Decent money. I can win it – I bloody will, unless some bastards manage to stop me.'

We walked to where our cars were parked. Travis had a VW 1500 station sedan, not new, not old, but a good car. I learned long ago not to judge a man by his wheels. We used our cars as shelter against the cold wind. Travis told me he'd heard about me in Brewer's gym, where he worked out with some boxers I knew.

'They say you're fair dinkum,' he said.

'There's no higher praise.'

'What would it cost to hire you as a bodyguard for a week? I mean all up – expenses and everything?'

I told him.

'Phew, that's steep, but I can manage it, just.

'Whoa,' I said. 'Bodyguarding you against what, exactly?'

'Who knows? Spiked drinks, assault, accidents. I'll be the favourite or near enough. The betting's going to be huge. I've heard some whispers, nothing specific, but … shit happens.'

'You're talking about a week at Willow Bend?'

'Right. I've hired a caravan. We go down there and train for a week. I need to get used to the atmosphere and the track. D'you know anything about running, apart from what your uncle did?'

'I ran a bit at school and in the bloody army.'

'You could appear to be my trainer. Do you good. Get a bit of the flab off, not that there's that much.'

The idea appealed to me. A holiday in the country. How hard could it be? I told him that I charged a substantial retainer but I'd waive that in return for him paying the expenses. I said I'd judge my total account according to whether he won or lost.

He laughed. 'Wow, that means I'll be paying full whack, because I'm a sure thing,'

We shook hands on the arrangement. I didn't tell him what life had taught me early on – that there's no such animal as a sure thing.

*

Travis towed the Nova caravan and I drove my own car. I had friends in Braidwood I planned to visit after the Gift had been run. The drive to Willow Creek went smoothly, although traffic thickened up as we got close to the town, with people involved in the agricultural exhibits and sideshows arriving early to set up. It was a small place and, like other towns in the area, had become known for its historical associations, arts and crafts, including a bijou brewery, and cafés and restaurants. As an entrant in the race, Travis got a prime spot in the caravan park. I left the Falcon close by and carried my overnight bag to the Nova.

I was surprised to see that Travis had laid on a couple of beers to welcome me to our temporary home.

'Last one before the race,' he said. 'Dry as a bone from now on, not for you of course.'

'I'll make it easy for you,' I said. 'I won't drink in here. Outside will be my business.'

'Fair enough. Thanks, Cliff.'

He was an easy man to like. Clean and neat in his habits, as I found, sharing a tight space with him. He had a good sense of humour and one of the crucial attributes of likeability: he knew when to talk and when to keep quiet, and especially when to tell a story to complement one of yours and when to shut up and let it ride.

The weather was kind; it can be cold there at that time of the year, but we hit a mild spell that looked like lasting until the big day. After a long time in Sydney I enjoyed the country air. The town was in festive mood and the show got underway with the usual attractions. No boxing tents though, which was something I always missed at city and country shows.

I mentioned this to Travis on our second night as we were having dinner in a café. I was having steak and chips, he was on a salad with no dressing and grilled fish. I had a local red wine, he had mineral water.

'Did you ever take a glove?' he asked.

'I did once, at the Sydney Show, just before I went into the army. Jimmy Sharman Junior's tent. I'd just started to drink and was a bit pissed and this big blackfella knocked me on my arse. Didn't last a round, didn't get the money.'

He'd been getting tense and I thought the story would amuse him but it didn't. I decided that was a good thing – he didn't like to hear about losing.

*

Travis handled all the administrative arrangements himself, unlike some of the runners who appeared to have trainer-managers. We trained on the big Willow Creek cricket ground where the story was that Don Bradman was the only man to ever have hit a six. That was as a teenager back in his brief country cricket days.

There were several closely mown strips on the oval that resembled the actual race track. Third time out, very early in the morning, I took my place with a stopwatch while Travis set himself. Something caught my eye and I held up my hand.

'Hold it!'

'What?'

I'd noticed a different colour in the grass about halfway down the strip as the light caught it. We inspected the spot and saw that the turf had been disturbed and there was a soft patch that would subside when a speedy foot hit it.

'Told you,' Travis said. 'You've got good eyes.'

We relocated. There was plenty of room on the oval and I inspected the ground carefully from then on. We fell into the routine of me setting off as a mock front marker and him having to catch me, which he did easily at first and less easily a bit later as I got into the swing of it.

'That Bradman story's bullshit,' Travis said the night before the first heat. 'I could hit a fucking six there off the right ball.'

'Easy, mate,' I said. 'A bit of a temperamental edge's a good thing, but don't go sour.'

He grinned. 'Fuck you. How'd you go after five days without a drink?'

'Not too good.'

We were sitting under the caravan canopy drinking coffee. Travis was toey but yawning, after a hard day's training. I was fresh after a swim in the river. Suddenly there was an odd noise, a grinding sound. I jumped up in time to catch one of the aluminium rods that supported the heavy canopy as it collapsed towards where Travis was sitting.

'Jesus! Those fuckers,' Travis snarled.

Together we inspected the damage. Two of the rods had been partly sawn through, leaving sharp edges. If they had caught Travis on the way down...

'See what I mean?' he said.

*

The bookies were there in strength, offering all kinds of odds on who'd make the final and the placings in the heats. I put ten bucks on Travis to win the Gift, but as he'd won his first heat and came a close second in the next, he was sure to start at a short price, if not as favourite. Although his slot as a back marker would have a bearing.

I wondered about that second placing. From having worked with him and watched other runners I was pretty sure he'd eased up in the heat and I asked him about it.

'I fucked up,' he said. 'Meant to come in third but that bugger Jacko Philips must've had the same idea and edged me out. Would have looked too obvious to really slow up and fourth was death.'

'This is to get better odds, is it? Are you betting?'

'Me? No. Can't afford it. I was angling for a lighter penalty but it didn't work. I'm off five yards.'

'Can you make that up?'

'Blood-oath I can. Put a few bucks on me, mate.'

'I have already, but I thought you weren't quite as sharp in our last session as you had been.'

He tapped the side of his nose. 'I told that journo who interviewed me I was tapering and he bought it. But … you know, there's eyes everywhere in this game and stopwatches in pockets.'

'I've heard of swimmers tapering but I didn't think it applied to sprinters.'

'It doesn't.'

'Did you tell the journo about me?'

He grinned. 'Just a bit. For colour.'

'And I thought boxing was dodgy.'

'This is the dodgiest, maybe along with the dogs. That's one of the reasons this could be its last gasp.'

*

The day of the race the local paper carried a story about Travis and how his bodyguard had averted several suspicious 'incidents'. His odds shortened so that he became virtually unbackable and odds on the other runners became correspondingly generous. I wasn't happy about the publicity, especially as it carried a photograph of me I hadn't been aware had been taken. I wished Travis luck and picked an unobtrusive spot to watch the race from.

The day was perfect and the crowd was large and noisy. The white-painted track lines stood out against the shaved-down green grass. In keeping with the traditional theme, the starter and other officials were decked out in nineteenth-century costume and there was a tape at the finish rather than the modern finishing line apparatus.

A 100-metre sprint by top athletes, even on a grass surface, is over in under ten seconds. Travis was on his back mark in the middle lane. He was quick out of the blocks and shot away, crouched initially and only coming upright as his speed increased. He was in the lead at the halfway point but Philips, the man who'd out-foxed him to take third place in the heat, hauled him in and beat him by a matter of inches.

I consoled Travis as we walked back to the caravan after the ceremony.

'What happened?' I said.

'Fucking cramp at the eighty-metre mark. Shit happens.'

Travis appeared crestfallen and I gave him a substantial discount on my fee. He wrote me a cheque and we shook hands. I packed up my stuff and headed off to my car for the drive to Braidwood. When I got there I found the battery had gone flat and it took me a while to find someone with jumper leads to get it started. Then I realised I'd forgotten to pack *The Playmaker*, the Tom Keneally novel I'd been enjoying .

I left the Falcon ticking over to charge the battery and headed back to the caravan in the gathering gloom. I approached from the rear and heard voices as I got close. Travis and another man were sitting under the repaired canopy and I heard the pop of beer cans.

Well, why not? I thought. *Camaraderie among athletes.*

I was about to step up when I heard Travis give a self-satisfied laugh. 'Would you believe, Jacko, I got ten-to-one on you and I had fifteen hundred down.'

'Shit, that means with half of the purse as agreed, you've finished up ahead of what you'd have got if you won.'

Travis laughed again. 'Right, but you never can tell. It was going to one of us and this made sure we both won. And you've got the glory, mate. I've pulled this stunt or something like it before but I reckon this was my last chance.'

'What about that minder? Good touch, the effect on the odds and that, but he didn't suss you?'

'I thought he might be onto me at one point, after the heat, but he let it slide. The accident sucked him in. He loved being part of a big sports scene. An athletics tragic is what he is.'

I stood there, seething, in the gathering darkness. I wanted to go in and flatten the pair of them but Travis was right. I'd let myself be seduced by the ambience, the atmospherics.

Fuck them both, I thought, and went back to my car.

*

The cheque bounced of course, but I had a good time with my people on their Braidwood farm. And his scheme didn't benefit Travis. The caravan jack-knifed on him at a bend on his way back and it and the VW went over a very long drop. It took two days to find the site and winch Travis up. From the state of the body they said he must have died instantly. That was lucky.

The Mango Tree

PM Newton

After thirty years, the only thing Sergeant Crotty still liked about being a policeman was the time he spent getting paid for not being one.

He calculated all the possible ways to earn leave. He worked all the public holidays and the late shifts. He took all the after-hours callouts, even when he had to find a payphone and make the calls himself: the anonymous informant reporting kids in cars was reliable standby. An hour to drive out there, an hour to tool around some of the back roads and an hour to drive back. Peace. Quiet. Away from her.

So far, his personal best was scoring three and a half months of leave in one year. He had spent hours on those long quiet night shifts diligently working out rates, pro ratas, allowances and time-in-lieu. There had been nothing else to do.

Murra at night was a peaceful place. A small coastal town balanced between a muddy river and a steep, dark beach studded with rocks. It was not a destination for holidaymakers: they drove further north to Coffs, or pulled off the highway a few hours south at Port. In fact, they only ever caused Crotty problems if they managed to jam themselves under a truck somewhere on the highway that joined the two towns. Not that he minded – a fatal was good for a few hours overtime, looking after the scene until the detectives arrived from the north or the south, depending on which side of the bridge the incident occurred.

Surfers found no joy in Murra. The breaks on both sides of the Murra River mouth were ordinary; the abrupt shore drew waves up late, high and mean. The damage done to body and board by the rocks beneath the foam deterred most surfers after one session. And if it didn't, Sergeant Crotty could extend the unwelcome with dark looks at bald tyres and the threat of a ticket for unroadworthiness.

There was fishing, for those brave and lucky enough to make it through the river mouth. Happily for Crotty, Murra had dropped off the senior brigade's caravanning itinerary after four pensioners flipped their tinnie one bright morning half a decade ago. Three days later the rip deposited a single body well down the coast – the others must have wound up feeding fish instead of catching them. These days, those few retirees who did come for a rest on the banks of the Murra contented themselves with catching twitchy flatheads among the mangroves in the upper reaches of the river. Sometimes Crotty joined them, piloting a small boat he'd bought cheap in an estate sale. He wasn't much interested in fish but he had a big esky and he kept it brimming with home brew. Best of all she hated it and never came.

These features combined to make Murra the best posting Sergeant Stan Crotty had ever had.

It should have made him happy.

It didn't.

Anger was a way of life. He'd forgotten what it felt like not to burn. He hated the job. Accumulating those hours he could not work and still get paid was a victory, but it barely diluted the anger.

Those of his colleagues who turned their mind to him thought Crotty the laziest policeman they'd ever known, and would have been astounded to know just how diligent he was in maintaining the dystopia he'd created for himself in Murra. Crotty had no illusions about his abilities, but he was dogged. And he'd taken the time to learn about the things that mattered to him. And now it was paying off.

He'd earned an assortment of leave – annual, long service, special – that would deliver him to the day he would leave permanently. That was in two years, five months and three days. A Tuesday.

Not for Stan Crotty the option of cashing in his entitlements, adding to a lump sum or rolling it over. No. He'd take every hour of leave he could, at half-pay, and only when he'd used up every drop would he officially retire. Until then, he planned to sit in his subsidised rental unit, with its view of the river mouth and the reef, brew his beer and ignore her. He calculated he could spend eighteen months without answering a phone, wearing a uniform, attending a call, or talking to a member of the public. And there was nothing they could do about it. He'd checked.

He imagined their fury and it warmed him.

What happened after, when it would be just him and her and they'd have to find somewhere else to live, he tried not to think about. When he did, it was a hot wind whistling through the flames of his rage…

Until that day, he'd go on much as he had. Friday nights were the best: a quick run through town before the game started, just to show his face. Then he'd call in that he was heading to Upper Murra on a report of kids in cars and he'd be out of radio contact. After that it was home along the back roads, parking in the garage and pulling down the door.

He kept a radio on the table by his chair, next to his beer, just in case. If anyone above the rank of Sergeant was hunting him up, he'd know. Beer in hand he'd settle into his chair and scratch his balls through his red nylon shorts.

Crotty didn't see her anymore. He noticed the cracks in the linoleum floor but he didn't see her sitting at the kitchen table. As the referee blew his whistle Sergeant Crotty wondered if he could have them pay for new lino. He made a mental note to look up the regulations about it tomorrow. There'd have to be a form somewhere.

*

Win watched her husband scratch his balls. A serpent of disgust slid through her bowels.

Her wet, sticky eyes gazed at the man she had lived with for more than thirty years. With his large head and veined skin, there was no trace left of the boy he'd been at eighteen: tall, silent, big-boned and ginger-haired, fresh from the wheat field. He'd carried huge bags without raising a sweat, arms like pink hairy hams. She remembered how their strength had excited her, how his big square hands had fumbled her, his nervousness inferred as tenderness. It had been an illusion.

Herself, she'd been the daughter of a local cop, which meant a childhood of itinerancy as one posting followed another. One dusty town bleeding into the next across the far west of New South Wales until, in her early teens, they'd hit the outskirts of a *city*. Only a couple of years there before they were transferred again. She'd eventually turned up in his town, a speck in the wheat belt, with all the knowledge two years in a suburb and a few evenings in a panel van at the drive-in could confer. Stan's initial hesitancy had been followed by a burst of instinct, of force that had felt manly to her after the tinkering of boys.

She thought she knew what she was getting.

She did not.

Win watched him. Bolted upright to his chair, glaring at the TV. The farm boy long gone. Now with the bright bitterness of hindsight she didn't think that boy ever really existed but in her own silly, scattered head. His strength had come from rage even then. But a young man's rage, full of potential, lacking only the direction she could supply. These days she still saw an angry man, purple cobwebs in his nose and cheeks. The fists still threatened.

Stan never hit. Too cunning for that. Bruises could convict. Same as he never yelled, no reports for the neighbours to make, no profile to build up. Instead he raged quietly. Not even directing it at her, but about her, in front of her. He abused and insulted, spat out his hate for her, for other people, for his workmates, his job, his life. The menace of violence that never came, a storm that would not break though the barometer sank lower. He would drop into a deeper intensity, massive fists like a pair of ripped-out hearts, clenching and unclenching over the arms of his chair.

She was proud that her rage was not hidden. She cursed and cried out, let the neighbours think what they like. She pushed and provoked and she punched. Stan was bigger, stronger, angrier; she could be meaner, nastier, drunker.

Win favoured a sweet yellow Fruity Lexia, iced in a long glass, applied in generous quantities between the hours of waking and passing out. She topped up now as she watched him watching TV.

'Stupid, pissed and angry.'

These were Jackie's last words before she slammed the door and moved to Sydney.

Their son had gone a year later. Not too far, just to the mango tree in the backyard. He'd strung himself up with his father's police belt, a thick black leather basketweave that made a collar for his neck. The holster was empty; the gun spilt onto the grass below. He'd hung in the fat, humid night beneath sharp stars while inside they'd drunk themselves to sleep, booze pouring down their throats and vitriol out their mouths. Another night at home.

A neighbour spotted him at daybreak, dropped the kettle in the sink when the twisting figure took shape in the morning mist. Like a rotten pear, bloated on the branch but unable to drop. It took twenty minutes of pounding on the back door to wake Stan. By the time Win came to, they'd cut the boy down and borne him away.

Admin supplied Stan with a new belt, but it still creaked as it strained around his guts.

Though she'd missed it all that morning, she saw Paulie's face, blue above the black, every time the basketweave groaned. The clang of a kettle rang through her head whenever she thought of the boy; he hung before her eyes whenever she heard one whistling on the stove.

Win wanted to blame the young mother, new to Murra, to their street. She never understood Paulie. How he played with all the local kids.

Always had.

Never grown out of it.

Never had to.

Not until this young mother began to forbid her six-year-old to play with Paulie. Never said anything concrete. Not in so many words. Just made it obvious when she called her boy in from Paulie's game of street cricket, or made a scene if they thought to go bushwalking. The bitch made sure everyone knew. The whispers started then – and spread. They reached Win, not Stan. No-one would dare say it to Stan.

Win could admit that her boy had been slow. Like a more stupid version of his father, bereft of the anger. Paulie's had been a gentle slowness.

The memory spilt the wetness from her eyes. It hadn't been the boy's fault. *There wasn't the information in my day*, she comforted herself. Nobody had warned her. The bloody doctor had drank *with* her. Drank with her and Stan all through that stinking summer while she ballooned into a wet, white mass.

Her pregnancy with Paulie passed in a boozy haze, stranded in some remote dot in the far west of the state, a black and white town in a sea of red dust. The blacks drank what they could, where they could and it was called a bloody disgrace. The whites drank what they could in each other's homes and it was called *socialising*.

A town awash in alcohol. The old missions were models of alcohol and abuse. The whites tut-tutted when the 'mish' came through and trashed the pub or broke into the bottle'o before passing out on the riverbank. White society trashed themselves like civilised people – behind closed doors. And no one acknowledged the black eye, the split lip, the broken arm as parties rolled from house to house. An entire town content to drink as it cooked slowly under the sun.

Stan sat like a rock, massive hands curled around the arms of his chair, unmoving as the TV crowd roared.

'We live like coons,' she snarled at the back of his head, voice climbing, combing her mind for the worst insult. 'Like fucking coons.'

*

She was white noise: sometimes louder, sometimes softer, never tuning in, never making sense. Sober or drunk, she was static. His team scored but he felt no delight, it was a ritual to watch but the pleasure had dwindled long ago. If he didn't watch, what else would he do? Talk to her? Watch her melt into tears and mucus?

In all his additions and subtractions he'd never factored her in. She was there, like the hair that grew from his ears, repulsive but inevitable. Kindling for his anger. Ridding himself of her required action but he had replaced action with routine for so long now that he was incapable.

Half-time came: his cue to put on the blue shirt and make another lap through town, then out to the highway. By then it would be time to call in a vehicle-check, before announcing he was heading out to Mount Purgatory, report of cattle on the road.

He was an automaton. No thought required. He felt something swipe his thigh as he passed through the kitchen. It didn't break his stride.

*

She heard the car roar out of the backyard. Her emptying glass lay on its side, where it had fallen when he'd clipped the table on his way through, blind to whatever pain he might have inflicted.

The wine flowed off the table, a thin yellow stream joining another pool of liquid on the lino. She stared at it. She felt a warm moist burning in her crotch. She'd wet herself. A blowfly bumbled about, alternately beating its head against the seat of the chair before diving into the puddle with an angry sodden buzz.

Win rose with a wet slap, her skirt clinging her legs. The chair toppled backwards onto the kitchen floor, its crash lost in the screech of the screen door as she pushed through and out into the backyard.

The skirt climbed her legs as she staggered over the driveway; her bare feet left a ragged trail of prints on the concrete. The grass felt clean as she walked to the mango tree, a black umbrella that blotted out stars. She grasped the trunk, her forehead resting there, her fingernails raking at the uneven bark. Her noises were less than words and more than sobs, raw communication with the plant that had helped to murder her child. It stood mute and huge, ignoring her attempts to hurt it.

Not until her fingertips were torn open, the bark embedded deep inside, did she push away. Mosquitoes, thriving in the damp and the dark of the canopy, clouded her legs but were driven back by the stink. She stepped away, stumbled over her own feet, fell flat

THE MANGO TREE

on her back, stared into the thick weave of branches. Unmoved, it rose above her, while she lay like a beetle at its feet. It had grown taller and widened by three since it had killed Paulie. Rage at its abundant life straightened her limp limbs. Rolling to her knees she heaved up, purpose guiding her back towards the house. On her way, she noticed.

He'd left the garage door open.

*

The radio squawked for his attention as he backed the Police Truck out. 'Whale in the bay.' A long time since he'd heard that call sign, but the meaning hadn't changed. Top brass, driving north up to Coffs, passing through his town for an unannounced drop-in. Crotty roared out of the yard and planned his intercept on the turn-off from the highway – he was up high in the truck so they'd never see his shorts. He grasped the handset and prepared a pretext. Somewhere out of town, an excuse to nod at the brass, then drive on and out and watch their tail lights disappear before he returned home.

*

It was unfamiliar territory. She knocked her knees and shins against the boat trailer before her eyes grew wide enough to navigate. No light. She couldn't risk a light. The boat, a pathetic tin can with a lawnmower engine stapled to its arse, seemed bigger in here, propped up on its dented trailer, all sharp edges and bruising corners. She rubbed at her injured legs and glared at it.

She forgot the mango tree.

The boat was his typical escape. He'd had others. Lawn bowls had folded after she'd gatecrashed the socials. With that she'd guaranteed he couldn't hide in plain sight. More private gatherings had shrivelled and died. Murra was a small town; she could always find him. Clandestine poker games hadn't lasted. He was too stupid, too poor and too mean. She considered this latest bolthole. Circled it like a cat preparing to mark its territory.

As she passed along the back wall she ran her bleeding fingers over the necks of glass bottles. Pyramids of undrunk bottles collected for no apparent purpose. Her hand closed on one.

'I launch the SS *Shit for Brains*.'

The bottle smashed over the engine, showering her with the malty liquid, leaving her grasping the jagged neck like this was a bar brawl and she was preparing to attack. The next five she pelted like rocks at the side of the boat until the glass drove her naked feet back. The ten after that she hurled like grenades into the belly of the boat. She panted and her arm ached and tiny needles of pain peppered her feet. Despite her flagging strength the pyramid was noticeably smaller. She pressed the sole of her foot against the sloping side of the pile and the glass cooled her fiery skin.

With a final heave she sent the pyramid tumbling, a cascade of foam shattered around the tyres of the trailer.

Stopping to catch her breath, she squatted on a canvas-covered lump. A round metal lid bit into her thighs. Win flipped the canvas back and saw the twenty-gallon drum beneath her. Standing, she dragged the canvas off – drum after drum revealed itself.

The first drum she dragged outside. This was bounty to be shared; there was enough to go round. She screwed the lid off and rolled it on its side, all the way to the mango tree. Her feet tingled as the fuel found the wounds in her feet. She danced a drunken jig across the winding river she made and by the time she got the drum to the tree it was all but empty. Resolute now, she doubled back, rolled a second drum to join the first, not taking off the lid until it was safely wedged against the trunk.

It was right that they should be joined: the two murderers of Paulie.

Not one tear. He'd shed not one tear for the boy. She'd make him cry now.

Drum after drum she opened and tipped over, only vaguely directing the stream of fuel: this one towards the trailer, this towards his home-brewing station. The floor grew slick, the air chromed her throat and delighted her brain. She giggled.

Cigarette lighter in hand she stepped back. The mango tree shone silver under the rising moon. She trailed the fumes of fuel with her, oiling the air, took off her shirt and stuffed it into the open drum, leant forward and her breasts swung heavy, nipples shrinking from the night air.

The flame leapt from her fingers.

*

He saw the light from the fork in the road. The dirt track ran down to the oyster leases where the moon shone hard on the river. The bitumen turned away and climbed the hill to town. The glow was yellow.

The siren summoned the bush fire brigade to action. By the time they'd heard it, it would all be over.

His siren was silent. He swung into the backyard. The tree was ablaze. A white furnace of flame ran from the tree to the garage where the roof was buckling, sucking down.

Between them both danced a figure, a pagan goddess, a human wick. Whirling, streaming with fire, it ran to him. He doused the headlights and ground the gears, but with a thump the flame launched onto the hood of the truck. Crotty had a glimpse of a skull, white light glowing in its eyes, its mouth, then it slid from view. He found reverse and roared backwards.

*

The note on the front door of Murra Police Station seemed to have been typed hastily. It was laminated though, and that gave it the look of something permanent.

> *Murra Police Station is unmanned until further notice. Please use the speakerphone to your right and you will be connected to the closest operational Police Station.*

Inside, Stan Crotty sat in the charge room, feet on the counter. He studied the departmental policies on compassionate leave with a frown. But then, every bit counted. He made some notes. When he turned to the section on stress leave a slow smile spread across his face. He would need the calculator for this one.

50

Thirteen Miles

Michael Caleb Tasker

He pulled over and looked left to the lake. The air was heavy with the morning's mist and he breathed heavily and rubbed his head with the palm of his hand. The humidity made everything damp to the touch.

He had seen her truck twice in three days. Early Sunday morning when he drove to Watson's café for breakfast, her black pickup truck was parked out front and he blinked as if waking from a dream and then drove all the way around Ten Mile Lake.

Monday and Tuesday he drove past the landing at the lake several times and in the evenings he drove past the Windy Water Motel hoping to see her. He got lucky Tuesday night. He saw her truck on the highway and followed from a ways back until she turned into the motel. By the time he caught up she was at the door to her room, a long black shadow going through the door.

The blanketed lake looked peaceful, quiet, maybe a little smothered. It was still early. The fog would not lift for a few hours, if at all. This time of year it was hard to tell. He got out of the car and went to the lake's edge, knelt down and splashed the cold water on his face and smiled.

It would be best to see her soon, get it over with. His throat became dry and his skin warm. He shook his head and went back to his car. He sucked on his lower lip and stared at the lake and thought about her. She would be out there all day, on the lake, looking.

*

He watched Thompson's boat come in. Her pickup was next to Thompson's in the dirt parking lot. She had used him last year as well. The boat drew a small, clean wake behind it and he squinted but could not see her. He slapped slowly at a mosquito on his arm, missed it and slid off the hood of his car and walked down to the dock. He stood on the wood planks, but did not go out over the water. Down the shore a tourist winched a beat-up tin can of a powerboat onto the back of a new truck. They started coming to the lake about the same time as the mosquitoes.

Thompson's boat came to the end of the dock and he watched Thompson jump out and secure it, tying it fore and aft. Thompson held up a hand to help her out and she took it roughly and jumped onto the dock. The two spoke.

She looked up and saw him. He thought she would have made a hell of a poker player. She walked along the dock, her steps sure, quiet and catlike. He tried to decide if he should smile at her. It didn't seem right.

She stopped and looked up at him. She had aged a lot in the year. The lines on her forehead looked like they had been carved with a thin chisel and she had cut her grey hair very short. But mostly it was around her mouth that her age showed. He wondered what she'd looked like when she was twenty. Pretty damn good.

'Deputy Marlin,' she said. 'It's been a while.' She kept her hands in the pockets of her yellow slicker.

He tried to smile kindly. 'How've you been, Mrs Lange?'

'You're from these parts, right?' she asked.

'Born and raised.'

'Then answer me this. The lake is four miles wide and thirteen miles long. Why is it called Ten Mile Lake?'

He watched her face. When he was a kid he'd wondered the same thing and always got a lot of silly answers. He didn't think he should give one to her.

'I don't know.'

She nodded. 'That seems to be the general state of mind around this fucking place.'

He looked to the lake as though it would clear the air.

'Will you be staying a while?' Marlin asked.

'As long as it takes.'

'What's he getting out of this?' He nodded towards Thompson, back on his boat, turning it around, going over to the other side of the lake.

'Seventy bucks a day and a sense of civic duty.'

'You still think I didn't do anything.'

'Not enough. Not for me.'

'You looked the whole lake twice over last year. So did we. There's nothing out there.' He looked out at the lake and it disappeared into itself.

'You think I'm wasting my time?'

'I don't know, Mrs Lange.' He moved his feet along the wood of the dock. He felt like he might fall in the lake and checked to make sure he was still over the land. 'I really don't know. I just worry.'

'Well, don't.' she said. 'You've gotten old this year.'

He smiled and she walked past him. She was much smaller than him but she seemed tall and he watched her walk. When he was a teenager he would have killed for a swagger as hard as hers.

She drove away and Marlin stood on the dock alone. He looked at the water and stepped off the dock, back onto the solid ground. His skin was clammy. She was right. He had gotten old this year.

*

It still got dark early. He drove home and took the long way, past the motel. Her pickup sat outside her room and through the curtains he saw the lights of the television. He guessed she was not paying it too much attention.

He turned onto the lake drive and started for home. He drove slowly. He stopped in front of his house and from the road he saw Carol inside, moving through the kitchen. Flashes of her black hair as she passed by the window. She stopped at the sink and Marlin saw her lips move. She was singing. He hadn't heard her sing in over a year. Hadn't seen her smile much either. He thought about Mrs Lange and chewed at his bottom lip. He bit away dried flesh and tasted the blood and when Carol looked up and out the window, he froze.

She could not have seen him; it was too dark out. He started the car again and drove away. He went halfway around the lake and then out past Dawson's Valley. The asphalt became gravel and then dirt that whipped hard at the undercarriage of his car. A road sign warned that the roads were not serviced during the winter months and he slowed down.

He stopped at a chain that ran across the road. He took down the *Road Closed* sign and put it in his boot. The chain was held closed with a pair of handcuffs so anyone could open them with a regular key and he unlocked the chain, wrapped it around a tree, locked it again. He wondered why they bothered with the handcuffs. No-one ever came out here but Marlin. Teenagers with girls or dope went somewhere with a lake view.

The road stopped after ten miles and he got out and walked through the trees. The beam from his torch bounced over the woods like a drunken horsefly. He started to sweat.

A heavy tree had fallen across the path long ago. Now it was covered with moss and ferns grew out of it. There was nothing on the other side of the tree and Marlin sat on it, his sweat cooling on his skin, and looked around, played the beam of his torch here and there and at nothing at all. It was dead quiet. He guessed no one had been there for a very long time.

When he was a teenager he'd come out to the fallen tree to smoke. Left the lake views for the other guys. When he started seeing Carol in the middle of his divorce he'd come out to the tree to hear himself think. Now he thought about Mrs Lange. He was surprised to find himself glad she was back.

*

The mosquitoes were getting worse. Even early in the morning, while it was still cool from night, Marlin felt them buzzing over the lake. He sat in his car at Thirteen Mile Point and looked down on the lake and waited for Thompson's boat. It would come. Sooner or later, she would come.

He got out of the car and rubbed insect repellent into his arms and neck. He stood high over the water and looked around. Years ago Carol had taken him to Thirteen Mile Point and they'd made love for the first time. He remembered her swollen, smiling lips; they always looked bruised and raw. Born and raised a few miles away, but he'd never known about Thirteen Mile Point. It was only good at sunrise. Not many people had the patience for a sunrise. He wondered how many men Carol had taken there over the years.

Thompson's boat came from the south. It moved slowly. It came head on towards Marlin and turned. They had covered a lot of ground in a week.

She stood holding a gunwale. Her neck was straight and smooth. Marlin liked the look of her tight blue jeans. He saw the dive tanks in the boat. He didn't know she could dive. She didn't do any diving last year.

They came back at him. A mosquito buzzed in his ear and he rubbed the insect repellent into his ears and along his cheeks as he watched Thompson's boat. They were doing a typical search and rescue, grid by grid. Marlin had taught Thompson how to do it properly last year.

Marlin looked at the clouds and felt the coming of the rain in the wind. He got back in his car and sat. He watched the boat head back south and keep going. They would be done for the day. Thompson wouldn't let her search with the weather turning bad.

He picked up three coffees on his way to the landing and was waiting with them in a cardboard tray when the boat came in. He walked out along the dock towards them and swallowed. His throat was too dry and he had to force his steps forward.

'Mrs Lange,' he said.

'Deputy Marlin.' She stepped off the boat and stood close to him.

Thompson jumped off and stood behind her, smiling. 'Hi there, Rick.'

'You want a coffee?' Marlin asked.

'I always do.' Thompson took the coffee and stood waiting.

Marlin looked at the clouds over the lake. There was still time before the rain.

'Find anything today?' Marlin asked. He gave her the other coffee.

'No,' she said. 'But we're just getting started. Thompson's got a new radar. State of the art. By the time I'm done looking I'll know everything there is to know about this fucking lake.'

He nodded and looked at his feet. The dock felt slick out over the water.

'You sure got pluck, Mrs Lange.'

'Pluck?'

'Pluck,' he said. 'Like fortitude.'

'I know what it means, Deputy. Just didn't think you were old enough to use that word.'

Other fishing boats were coming in. Some were still far out and Marlin thought they would be caught by the weather. Thompson always had a good eye for weather. First in, first out.

'What if you don't find anything?' he asked.

'Then I'll look somewhere else.'

'And what if you do find something?'

'Then I'll know.'

He nodded. He looked at the water. It was very still and he frowned. 'You sure that's the best thing?'

'I have to know, Marlin. It's my son.'

The rain came and it hit the lake and Marlin thought about what Carol looked like naked, that time at Thirteen Mile Point.

*

He came in the door and took off his raincoat. He could smell chicken but knew Carol would have eaten earlier, without him. He listened and heard the radio in the kitchen and the rain outside and the blood in his ears.

'You're home late again.' Carol came from the hallway. Her face looked like it had been scrubbed hard. He wanted to kiss her.

'Sorry. I had to work back.'

'Don't apologise. I'm used to it.'

'There was an accident on Route 106. Some tourist wrapped his car around a tree and then walked off into the woods. Not a scratch on him, but he has no idea which way is up.'

He followed her into the kitchen. It was warm in the house and she wore old yoga clothes. They fit her well.

'I made dinner.'

'I can smell it.'

'I already ate.'

He nodded and watched her bend over to open the oven. She took out the baking dish and he could smell the garlic on the chicken.

Marlin moved up behind her and wrapped his arms around her waist. He kissed her neck. Her shampoo was expensive and smelled like it. He pressed his face into her black hair and she felt small in his arms. The muscles in her back were tensed and her arms were still. He tried to take her hands in his and they were cold. She started to shake slightly and he felt her chest gasp quietly for air, sudden and sharp and crying.

He held her and kissed the back of her head.

That night he lay in bed and listened to her sleep, to the soft, warm sound of her breath. The rain had stopped, but when the wind blew it still fell in the trees out front of the house. He got out of bed and she stopped breathing. He knew she was awake. He got dressed in the hallway and went outside and sat in his car.

Marlin looked at his watch. The sun would be up in two hours. He drove out to the Windy Water Motel but Lange's pickup wasn't there. He wondered who she was staying with and drove around the lake and then out past Dawson's Valley. He sat on the fallen tree until the sun came up and then he went in to work.

*

The lake was quiet, empty. The morning mist hung close to the black surface of the water. It gave Marlin the creeps. He thought it looked like a black hole that would suck a man down in a second and leave nothing but a calm, soft ripple that would fast disappear. He didn't know how people could go out over it day after day. But they did.

Her son had been missing over a week, but no-one had really noticed. Not until his backpack washed up on the shore, a good spread of blood on it. Then they realised he was gone. Then they worried. Soon Marlin found part of an outboard motor, banged up badly. Most people figured Jason Lange had gotten drunk again, taken a midnight ride again, and had crashed and gone under, swallowed up by the lake. Marlin suggested he might have pushed one button too many and just left town, but no-one believed that. So they searched the lake. Marlin ran the whole show from dry land. Born and raised just down the road, but nothing scared him more than that lake.

Nothing was found. No body, no more boat parts and again Marlin suggested maybe Jason Lange had left town. But his mother came and one look at her face and he knew they had to look again. So they did and she stood by and watched carefully. She had asked Marlin why he didn't go out on the water.

'That's a lot of lake,' he had answered. 'I can see it all better from up here.'

'Then I'll go.'

'We already looked twice. The boss won't let us take up more time or money.'

'I'll do it myself.'

And she stayed until the season ended and the weather became too bad and Thompson told her half the lake would freeze over for winter.

Now she was back out on the water, looking again. Slower, more carefully. She would know that lake better than anyone soon enough. She would know everything about it.

Marlin watched the lake silently. Though it was still foggy, the weather was fine. He knew she would be out there all day. She would stay out in a storm if Thompson let her. He thought of her face, grown old but still striking, and he bit his lower lip and thought she was tougher than hell.

*

He drove home along the lake and thought that now even the nights were muggy. He hoped Carol was still up, but it was late. It wouldn't matter if she were awake. She faked sleep as well as everything else. But at least she was singing again. Not around him, but it was something. He remembered her voice. He loved it almost as much as he loved her mouth.

Marlin turned away from the lake and went past the motel out of habit. Lange's pickup wasn't there. He drove by the motel most nights and it was hit or miss with her truck. She had made a friend. He smiled and thought she would be a good friend to have. She had loyalty in spades.

He saw her pickup under the streetlamp near his house. He looked in the truck as he went by and it was empty and lights were on in his living room window. Carol had let her in.

He guessed Lange was waiting for him and he didn't stop. Didn't even slow down. He didn't like the thought of Carol talking to her, but he liked the thought of walking in on it even less.

He went back to the lake drive and started around the lake. It was quiet and dark and he wondered why Lange would go to his house so late.

Because she needed to find her son. Nothing else mattered. Not to her.

Headlights shone in his rear-view mirror and when he looked again it was black behind him and the road was empty. Marlin eased down below the speed limit and cruised along, watching every now and again in the mirror. He went around the lake and saw the turn off for Dawson's Valley. He ignored it and kept going straight. Stayed close to the lake. Close to home. He wanted to go home to Carol.

*

They found something. He didn't know what, but by the way they moved around in the boat he knew they'd found something. Sweat ran down his back and he smiled. It was Thompson doing the diving. Marlin thought a man could see everything from Thirteen Mile Point. Sometimes too much. Thompson stripped down to his underpants and pulled on the wetsuit while Mrs Lange stared at the radar. The sky was clear and there was no wind, but the boat rocked. Something in the lake that couldn't be seen. Marlin shook his head.

Thompson fell back into the water and was swallowed up. Every now and then air bubbled up to the surface. Lange stood watching the radar. Her shoulders had become red with sunburn in the last few days. But it was a healthy sunburn that made her skin look smooth, made Marlin wonder what it would be like to touch.

The boat swung heavily as though being pulled down into the flat lake. Lange fell back and grabbed hold of the throttle and the boat shot forward. It motored south, full tilt and Marlin stood straight.

That fucking lake is haunted, he thought. Thompson's boat left a canyon of white water for a wake and finally circled to a slow stop and rocked back and forth and it was empty.

Marlin went to the water's edge, high over it and looked again. The boat was far away but he couldn't see Lange. He went to his car and opened his lockbox, the binoculars next to his gun. He took the binoculars and scanned the water and saw Lange floating, face down. He watched her thin body and she sunk a few inches and came back up. He waited, hoping for Thompson to surface.

He dropped the binoculars and ran down from Thirteen Mile Point and kept going along the shoreline. The water looked calm and quiet, but he didn't trust it. He got close to Lange and took off his heavy belt and his boots and jumped in the lake. He swam out to her and swallowed enough water to make his own lake. He pulled at her body, grabbed her belt and kicked back for shore. Her weight pushed him under and he tried to surface. He got a swallow of air and went down again and pulled her towards the land and felt the soft mud on the bottom. He thought it might suck him down.

Marlin turned Lange over onto her back and kept pulling. She breathed and he held her around the waist.

She grabbed his arm. Her nails dug in and she pushed him away.

'Get the fuck off me,' she said. 'Get away from me.'

She stood in the shallows and he held up his hands. She coughed and moved to the shore and leaned forward, her hands on her knees. Blood came from a cut on her forehead. She looked over at Marlin.

'I thought you couldn't swim,' she said.

'I can't.'

Out in the lake Thompson broke the surface. He looked around and saw them and waved happily.

'I'll drive you back to your motel,' Marlin said.

*

It was a clear morning. They were rare. There was more fog in the trees than over the lake. But the mosquitoes kept it from being too idyllic. He saw a few boats, but none of them belonged to Thompson. But they were out there. Maybe doing the east side of the lake, maybe anywhere. It was a hell of a lot of lake. He sucked on his lower lip and thought about pulling her ashore. Her body had been very firm, very tense. It reminded him of Carol.

He pulled onto the road and made a lap around the lake and checked in at the office. There was paperwork from the car accident earlier in the summer. The insurance company didn't want to pay out. He drank a coffee and looked out the window and put the paperwork aside for another day. It was too good a day for the office so he got back in the car and drove around the lake and then out past Dawson's Valley.

The mosquitoes were thick in the trees but the insect repellent was thick on his skin. Even still they buzzed in his ears. They could make a man loose his mind, he thought. Just the sound of them. The constant buzz that trapped a man's soul and sucked him down like that lake promised to do.

He sat on the fallen tree and stared at the earth and thought about Carol and thought about how she looked naked, her mouth wet and smiling, her black hair spread out as she laughed, that time at Thirteen Mile Point. Nothing was more beautiful.

Dead pine needles covered the ground he stared at. He looked at the ferns growing out of the fallen tree. Some had been flattened. He walked around and stopped, looking down at a shoeprint, a small one. He wondered who had been out there, sitting on the tree.

Marlin walked back to his car, followed by the mosquitoes. Thompson and Lange would be coming in soon. He wanted to be there. They would not find anything, not in that lake. He wanted to help her. Standing around was the only way he could think of.

She did not need any help, he thought. Not from him. Not from anyone.

He drove to the landing and waited. He parked next to Thompson's truck and looked around for hers. It wasn't there.

It was dark by the time he got home. Lange's pickup was in his driveway and he sat parked on the street watching it, watching his house.

He thought about Lange, in his house again, with his wife again.

*

Marlin sat on the hood of his car and watched the sun come up. It was a hell of a sunrise. Not many people had the patience for a sunrise. Fewer still knew how good it was at Thirteen Mile Point. Carol knew.

He remembered how Carol breathed wetly in his ear the first time they were together and how they lay in the bed of the county pickup and hoped for a sunrise. There wasn't one. Just the mist protecting the lake. He remembered how soft she was and he thought about Lange. There was nothing soft about her.

Marlin looked to the lake. It was too early for the mosquitoes to be out. The mist was burning away quickly and the lake was calm and quiet. He felt like it was watching him.

He remembered the way Carol laughed, her naked body shaking slightly, her black hair spread out over the Lange boy's chest, and he remembered hearing her sing while he watched them. It was the last time he heard her sing.

Postcard From Cambodia

Andrew Nette

The engine of Moss's 1990 Commodore started to play up thirty minutes past the first sign for Riviera. He ignored the burning smell, cajoled and caressed the vehicle's cracked dashboard, like a desperate jockey nearing the finish line.

Moss had bought the car for three hundred and fifty dollars from a hippy pet shop owner in Eden. He'd checked under the hood, with limited mechanical knowledge, and reassured himself everything was okay. He realised now he'd been too hasty to conclude the deal and get clear of the aroma of dog shit and marihuana that clung to the middle-aged love child.

When the burning smell got worse, Moss pulled off the road to an empty picnic spot, retrieved his black canvas bag from the back seat. He remembered the Smith & Wesson in the glove compartment, another impulse buy, wondered whether he should take it. He dismissed the idea.

He locked the car, set off on foot for the remaining ten or so kilometres into town, lit a cigarette as he walked along the roadside. The setting sun followed him in brittle yellow streams between the tall trees.

*

Moss chose the first motel he came to. A well-lit front office, rooms in a single story U-shape around a car park at the rear. The neon sign announced vacancies.

A bell tinkled as he entered the office. He stood at the counter, thumbed a stack of forlorn-looking fliers for local attractions, a nature walk, a historic railway bridge. Canned television laughter was audible in the back office. A middle-aged male with thinning brown hair and doughy features parted a curtain of yellow beads, gave Moss a sullen once-over.

'Help you?'

'I'd like a room for a couple of nights.'

'Fill out your details.' He passed a registration form and a key attached to a round piece of wood with the number 11 on it. 'How're you paying?'

'Cash.'

'I'll still need a credit card, just in case.'

'Don't have one.'

The man's eyes narrowed. He started to speak but Moss silenced him by placing a fifty-dollar note on the counter.

The man ran two fingers over the white stubble on his fleshy chin, pretending to consider the offer. He shrugged and pocketed the note.

'My car broke down about ten kilometres out of town. Who can I see about getting it towed in and repaired?'

'Hennessy's garage at the end of the main street, but he's shut till morning.'

'Where can I go to get a bite to eat?' Moss paused a beat. 'And some female company.'

The man licked his pale lips, smiled at the prospect of a fellow conspirator.

Moss placed another fifty on the counter.

*

Moss disliked arriving anywhere in the dark, the sense of disorientation and lack of control. He took his time walking along the main drag, getting his bearings. Mid-week on the cusp of winter, a couple of takeaway shops and the pub the only signs of life.

Most of the buildings were red brick. A few were older, beginning of the last century, the occasional art deco flourish. Built with logging money. A small country town populated by honest, hard-working souls, but poke hard enough or ask the right person, the sleaze wasn't far away. He'd got lucky. The hotel receptionist was the right person. It had been the same during his time in Asia. Even the friendliest place had an underbelly, a club, bar or house like the one the receptionist had told him about. And Riviera didn't seem that friendly.

Moss sat at the pub counter, eating a mixed grill, taking his time. A smattering of customers pretended to mind their own business, but couldn't help checking out the new arrival. The walls were covered with framed black-and-white photographs from the town's earlier days: horse-drawn carts hauling logs through the bush, groups of solidly built timber-cutters gazing at the camera, axes over their shoulders. He wondered where the name Riviera had come from. The town wasn't near the sea, not even a river. The photos supplied no clue.

He exited the pub into the chilly night, walked along the main drag, his breath making little clouds, until he found the side street. He passed a few businesses, some of them permanently shuttered, a large stone church set back on a wide lawn. Another few metres he saw the sign, the word 'Barons' in yellow neon letters.

He pushed open the metal door. Inside was all smooth surfaces and cheap stainless steel finishing. Classic rock from the speakers, cigarette smoke hung in the air, sport on a TV over the bar; the bright green playing field stood out in the dimly lit space. The only other customers were a clutch of men and a couple of young women at the end of the bar. The men paused, looked at Moss, went back to their conversation.

It took Moss a moment to register the presence of several other young females sitting around a glass table in a corner. They reminded him of girls at a school dance, awkward but alert, trying to look street smart beyond their years. Moss glanced at each in turn. His heart skipped a beat as he locked eyes and let his gaze linger on the tallest of the group. He noticed her brown skin and Asian features.

When the bartender approached, he nodded at the single beer tap, lit a cigarette, closed his eyes against the smoke. When he opened them, the tall girl was at his side.

'Got a light?' Shoulder length hair fell around her oval face, framed her large brown eyes. It was jet black except for a badly dyed stripe of purple.

Moss offered her his lighter.

She grinned. 'Got a smoke, too?'

He slid the packet across the bar towards her. She took two, lit one, put the other in the pocket of her denim jacket. She perched on the stool, placed a shoulder purse on the counter.

'Haven't seen you in here before?' she said, between quick drags on her cigarette.

'Haven't been in here before.'

'Passing through?'

'Yeah, something like that.'

'Consider yourself lucky.' She glanced around the bar before returning her gaze to him. 'Buy me a drink?'

Moss nodded at the bartender. She poured the girl a rum and Coke.

'What's your name?' She dabbed a finger in the condensation on the side of her glass as she spoke, made a circle of moisture on the bar top.

'Moss.'

'I'm Hannah.' She ground her cigarette out in the ashtray between them. 'Want some company, Moss?'

'Seems to me that decision's already been made.' He smiled to take the edge off his discomfort, suddenly self-conscious in his cheap leather jacket and old jeans.

'Dude, seriously, I don't have time for mind games.' She blew her cheeks out. 'It's not like anyone comes in here by accident.'

'I'll take your word for it.'

'So, you want some company or not?'

'Sure.'

She slid another cigarette from his pack, lit it.

'You want to do it here or somewhere else?'

'What?

'You want to fuck here? There's a room out the back, or somewhere else?'

There was nothing sleazy in the statement. She could have been talking about the weather or her favourite sports team.

Moss drained his beer. 'Let's go back to my motel.'

'You got to talk to Erskine, you want to do that.' She signalled over his shoulder.

He turned around just in time to see a man break away from the group at the end of the bar. The man's companions watched intently as their friend approached, faces grinning in anticipation, the joke at Moss's expense.

'I don't know you.' The man had a broad build, straw-coloured hair, cut short back and sides. 'Been in the Riviera long?'

'Just stopping in town for a few days while I get my car serviced.'

'Like it?'

Moss hesitated.

'Mate, I'm just fucking with you.' The man grinned. 'As my late father used to say, no names, no pack drill.'

Moss detected menace behind his jaunty demeanour, the life of the party and the unofficial enforcer.

'You want to take Hannah for some fun, yeah?' Erskine placed his arm around her narrow shoulders. She winced at the contact.

'You can pay her when you're finished. Do whatever you want, but no rough stuff. Any rough stuff, I'll find out and you'll answer to me. Understood?'

Moss nodded, stood up.

Erskine turned to go back to his mates, paused halfway.

'You crazy kids have a good time now.'

Male laughter accompanied them out of the bar.

*

It started to rain on the walk back. They ran the remaining several hundred metres, damp and out of breath by the time they reached the motel.

Moss closed the door after her, flicked a light switch. The fluoro tube in the pelmet above the double bed spluttered to life.

She threw her shoulder purse on the round laminated table, breathed deeply.

'I got to piss.'

Moss picked up a glass, took off its plastic wrapping. He lit a cigarette, sat on the edge of the bed and tapped the ash into the glass, the rain louder now. His fingers stroked the checked acrylic blanket as he thought about Thailand and Cambodia, other times, perched on the edge of a bed, waiting as a female he didn't know moved about in the adjoining bathroom.

He looked up at the sound of the door opening. Hannah stood, backlit by the bathroom light, naked except for her bra and panties. Only just out of her teens, but nothing remotely girlish about her body, the way her hip curved, the swell of her breasts as she placed her clothes in a bundle on one of the chairs.

She plucked the cigarette from his mouth with an exaggerated gesture, like something she'd seen in a movie, dropped it in the glass. She pushed him down and started to straddle him, her narrow fingers pulling at his belt.

'Stop,' Moss said, pushed her away.

A strand of black hair fell across her face. She bit her lower lip, made another attempt to unbuckle his belt.

'No.' Moss pushed her away, harder this time.

Her brow furrowed. 'I could give you a massage, get you in the mood…'

'No.'

She folded her arms over her breasts, fixed him with a determined look. 'What the fuck game you playing, man?'

'It's just…' Moss realised he hadn't planned what he was going to say. 'I'm tired. I had a long drive today.'

'So, what am I supposed to do? Walk back in the rain to the club.' She snatched a singlet from her pile of clothes, pulled it over her head. 'I'll be fucking soaked by the time I get there. It's even further to the caravan park.'

'Caravan park?'

'Where me and another girl stay.' She pulled on her tight black jeans one leg at a time. 'Not that it's any of your fucking business.'

'Don't worry, I'll pay you.'

'Bloody hell, you'll pay. I leave here without the cash, Erskine'll have my arse.'

'He your pimp?'

'Yeah, that and a lot of other things.'

Moss lit a cigarette. 'You don't have to go.'

'What do you mean?'

'Sleep here. In the morning, I'll give you whatever money you're owed. You can go. Erskine will be none the wiser.'

She paused, one arm in the sleeve of her white top, her large eyes narrowed suspiciously. 'What's your game, Moss, or whatever the hell your name is?'

'No game.' He held the cigarette pack out to her. 'I'm just more tired than I thought I was, okay? The room's dry and warm. Sleep here, I won't try any funny stuff. Promise.'

'I thought funny stuff was the reason you brought me here.' She took a cigarette, accepted his light. 'What the fuck, man, you're still paying, what've I got to lose?'

'Exactly.'

'Got anything to drink?'

Moss unzipped his canvas bag, pulled out a third-full bottle of bourbon, held it up for her to see.

'This do?'

She smiled her agreement.

*

Moss saw his pale aging features superimposed on the window. The rain came down at a hard angle on the empty carpark. Hannah slept in the bed behind him. The water on the window made streaking patterns on her face and exposed shoulder.

The worst time in prison was when it had rained. The drains overflowed, the rats came out, and the dead air was full of mosquitoes and the stench of cramped bodies. Everything was damp. For some reason, no-one was allowed out of the cells when it rained. And it rained a lot in Cambodia.

He and Rory had been sentenced to eight years each in Complex One, Prey Sar, for importing two kilos of ecstasy tablets from Thailand. Moss's idea: they'd sell the pills on Phnom Penh's backpacker party circuit, make some quick money, get out of Cambodia, where they'd been for six months. Rory wasn't sure he wanted to leave; he'd met a local woman, Chon, and was thinking of staying, but went along with the plan anyway, could always use the money.

Their partner in crime, Narridh, was a rich Cambodian kid Moss had met one night in a bar called The Heart of Darkness. When the police arrested them in possession of the tablets, Narridh's connections gave him protection. The cops offered the two foreigners a deal. Pay ten thousand dollars or jail. They didn't have the money so it was jail.

Moss had gone through Hannah's purse while she slept, found condoms, a twenty-dollar note, a few loose cigarettes, a mobile with no credit, and a creased, dog-eared postcard. On the front of the card was wide stretch of sandy beach, palm trees, calm blue water, with the words 'Welcome to Sihanoukville' in gold letters. Moss had been there, a deep-water port and popular tourist destination in the south of Cambodia. He flipped the postcard over, winced when he recognised the almost childlike handwriting, promising to take Hannah to Sihanoukville one day.

Chon had been born in a dirt-poor farming village near Sihanoukville, left at the very first opportunity, took the well-trodden path to Phnom Penh and a job as a bar girl. Rory had taken her home from one of the dives on Street 51; a week later he said he was in love with her.

Moss's needs were much simpler. But the nights Rory was out of town, the nights Moss had slept with Chon – their bodies slick from sex in the tropical heat, the ceiling fan slowly spinning above – changed that. He'd never met anyone like Chon. She had a hair-trigger temper but she also loved to laugh – a harsh, guttural sound that seemed too big for her relatively small size. She devoured everything in her path: food, drugs, men, life.

Halfway through their jail sentence, Rory was killed in a fight with another inmate over a stretch of floor space. The worst thing: part of Moss was glad his friend would never know.

After his release, Moss stayed in Phnom Penh long enough to sort out a new passport and enquire about Chon. The few people who remembered her said she'd left town soon after he and Rory had gone to prison. One of them, a worn-out bar girl with half a missing finger, told him Chon had gone to visit a relative in Melbourne, gave him an address.

When Moss got back to Australia seven years later, he looked up the address: a housing commission flat in Broadmeadows occupied by a Cambodian family. Chon, a distant relative, had stayed there long enough to have her baby, a daughter called Hannah. He tracked her up the Hume to Sydney before losing the trail.

Moss had better luck with Hannah. It took him a couple of years, searching between jobs, but he was able to pick up her trace through an old mate working in residential care. It was through him that Moss found out about Hannah's encounters with the law, the first time for shoplifting; the next, soliciting.

'What about your parents?' Moss had asked Hannah as he poured the last of the bourbon.

'Never knew my dad; Mum didn't talk about him.' Her was voice drowsy with alcohol and exhaustion. 'Mum was seriously fucked up.' The words flowed with the ease that comes when you talk to a complete stranger, someone you don't care about or think you'll ever see again. 'She used to dress me up, drag me to bars with her, a conversation starter to pick up men. Once she made me carry drugs for one of her boyfriends, this creepy wannabe-biker dude.'

'What happened to her?'

'She died.' She said it matter-of-fact, the pain long gone or covered over with more recent scars.

Moss swallowed, tried to sound casual. 'How?'

'It doesn't matter.'

The crumpled postcard said different.

*

Moss woke before she did, lay next to her in the dull grey light through the part in the curtain, looking for a resemblance.

After a while he reached out, shook her shoulder. She came awake slowly, opened her eyes, unperturbed at finding herself next to a stranger.

They took turns in the shower. As they were about to leave Moss handed her money, suggested breakfast before he went to see about getting his car fixed.

She shrugged, her wet hair like flowing tar. 'If you're paying, sure.'

He opened the front door, indicated for Hannah to go first. She stepped outside, froze.

'You kids sleep well?' Moss heard a male voice say.

It was the man from the bar last night, Erskine, only this morning he wore a police uniform.

On the other side of the police cruiser, out of harm's way, stood the receptionist. He grinned, amused at Moss and the girl's surprise.

'Get in the car, Han,' Erskine said calmly. 'I'll run you back to the park.'

She hesitated.

'I said get in the fucking car.' He watched her climb into the back seat of the cruiser. She sat very still, eyes straight ahead.

Erskine smiled, hitched his belt up, a move Moss knew was designed to draw his attention to the holstered gun on the cop's hip. Erskine's eyes were hidden behind wraparound sunglasses.

'Have fun last night?' said Erskine.

The motel's receptionist licked his lips, leered at the innuendo.

'Having sex with a woman must feel good, Eric, after all those years taking it up the arse in that shithole in Cambodia.'

Moss tried to cloak his surprise, failed if the look on Erskine's face was anything to go by.

'Yeah, we may be a small town but we still have Google. How many years did you do again? Seven, eight? Must have been a tough gig.' Erskine's brow furrowed in mock concern. 'How old are you? Thirty-five? Christ, man, you look fifty, beat up and wasted. Not that I'm surprised, what you went through, wipe a few years off any man's life. What are you doing here in Riviera?'

'Just having a look, free country after all.'

'No, mate, it's not. Not in this town.'

Moss reached into his leather jacket.

Erskine whipped his pistol out, held it two-handed, the barrel pointed at Moss's face. 'Easy, man.'

'Just getting my smokes.'

Erskine nodded, lowered the pistol slightly.

Moss lit up, offered the pack to Erskine.

'Thanks but no thanks.'

'You were saying?' said Moss, the nicotine taking the edge off his fear.

'I don't know what the hell you're doing here but I don't like it. I smell something on you and it's not her.' He gestured with his head at Hannah sitting in the back of the car.

'Des here says you were asking him about getting your car fixed. What's the problem?'

'Don't know, it stalled about ten kilometres out of town.'

'Okay.' Erskine breathed deeply, slid his gun back into its holster. 'You go to Hennessy's garage. Tell them I sent you and they're to give you priority. As soon as your car's fixed, fuck off out of here.'

Moss drew hard on the last of his cigarette as he watched the police car pull out of the carpark.

*

It was late afternoon when the Commodore was good to go. Moss had accompanied the mechanic, a beefy twenty-something male with red hair, to retrieve it. Half-way back into town Moss realised where he'd seen the man: one of Erskine's drinking mates from the previous evening.

Moss returned to the hotel to collect his things. The room hadn't been cleaned and Hannah's scent was still in the air.

He avoided eye contact as the receptionist prepared his bill, his heart beating faster, not sure he could control his temper if he had to look at that man's smirk one more time.

He threw his bag into the back seat, started the engine and floored it out of the motel car park.

Chon had never visited him or Rory in jail. Towards the end of his term, when it seemed he might just make it out alive, Moss wanted, more than anything, to talk to her. He eventually managed to get hold of a smuggled mobile phone, but before he could use it, the prison governor ordered the guards to raid all the cells – a crackdown on contraband. The guards confiscated every mobile in the joint, including his, burned them in a foul-smelling pile of plastic and circuitry in the prison courtyard. Soon after the governor hired a private company to install a mobile phone jamming system.

He kept the number for Chon, called it the day he was released. Moss wasn't surprised when he got a recorded message in Khmer telling him it was no longer in use. He never got to hear her singsong voice, her broken English phrases, again. He never got to tell her he knew she'd sold them out to the cops in return for avoiding jail time but he wasn't angry. He understood she was pregnant and just doing what was necessary to make sure she and the baby didn't end up in prison.

As Moss drove through the outskirts of Riviera, he remembered cradling Rory's broken head in his lap, the inmates pressed in a circle around them, the only sound the smack of truncheons as guards beat his friend's killer unconscious and dragged him away.

Moss did a sharp U-turn, headed back into town.

*

Moss got directions to the caravan park from an elderly woman walking her dog. He parked outside the entrance, went on foot, past the temporary visitors, looking for the long-stay residents.

He eventually found a pre-fab building in an isolated spot at the rear. A clothesline was strung up outside, flapping with brightly coloured pieces of female clothing. A tattered canvas awning covered the front entrance, several chairs arranged in a circle underneath. Soft drink cans and food wrappers were strewn in the long grass. The steady thrum of dance music was audible from inside.

'Hannah,' he said loudly, to make himself heard over the music. He rapped his knuckles hard on the side of the building. 'Hannah, you in there?'

The music stopped. He heard movement inside; a female, around Hannah's age, appeared on the other side of the fly screen door. He recognised her as one of the girls in the bar the night before.

'What do you want?'

'Hannah there?'

'It's okay, Stace,' came a voice.

'What are you doing here?' Hannah said, closing the screen door behind her. She wore the same clothes she'd had on that morning.

'Pack some stuff, we're getting out of here.'

'What do you mean *we*? Just because you buy me for a night and don't turn out to be a complete arsehole, doesn't mean you get to tell me what to do. I don't even know who you are.'

'I don't have time to explain it to you now. But your mum…' he hesitated. 'She would've wanted you to come with me.'

'What the fuck you know about my mum?' Hannah spat out the words, stepped away but her eyes didn't leave his.

Moss pinched the bridge of his nose, tried to find the right words but they wouldn't come. What could he tell her? He didn't know whether she was his, Rory's or someone else's. He'd only known Chon a short time – not at all, really. He didn't know anything.

'Hannah, I'll tell you everything, I swear,' he said, straining to keep the desperation out of his voice, worried it might panic her. 'But, please, just get some stuff. Let's get out of here.'

Hannah teared up, wiped them away with the sleeve of her top.

'Where?' She sounded resigned.

'Wherever you want.'

'The sea?'

'Sure, now come on, get some stuff.'

Moss took her by the arm, led her past the other woman, Stace. Inside was dark and cramped. Clothes lay everywhere, unwashed dishes piled in the sink. Moss found a plastic bag, gave it to Hannah. 'Put what you need in here.'

Hannah plucked several pieces of clothing off the floor, put on her jacket.

'You right?'

She sniffed, nodded. Moss couldn't read her face in the dimly lit space.

'Come on, then.'

'Hang on.' She moved a pile of clothes off a tattered recliner chair, until she found what she wanted, her shoulder purse.

Moss waited as Hannah and Stace hugged, engaged in a rapid-fire hushed conversation. Then Stace watched them leave, face pressed against the fly screen door.

Moss walked in silence to the car, scared to say anything in case she changed her mind, threw the plastic bag of clothes she'd collected in the back. She climbed into the passenger seat.

'You going to drive, drive,' she said. 'Let's get out of this shit hole.'

He kept to the speed limit through town, only picked up the pace when they passed the sign farewelling them from Riviera.

Hannah leant over, started twisting the nobs on the car radio. 'This thing work?'

'Don't know, never tried it.'

'Doesn't look like it.'

'We'll get a new one.' Taking one hand off the steering wheel, Moss fished out his cigarettes, lit two from the dashboard lighter, passed one to her. 'We need to put as much distance between Riviera and us as possible. You drive?'

'No.'

He reached in front of her, opened the glove box and withdrew a folded map, exposing the grip of his revolver. He pushed the weapon into the cavity, not sure whether Hannah had registered its presence, closed the glove box.

'You're on navigation detail.'

Hannah started to unfold the map, confused.

With one hand Moss re-adjusted the map so it was right-side up. 'Like this, okay?'

When Hannah didn't respond, Moss glanced at her. Her eyes were fixed on her side mirror.

He checked the rear-mirror. A white vehicle was closing on them. The word 'Police' visible across the bonnet in blue letters.

Erskine, thought Moss. Who had tipped him off? Hannah's friend from the caravan park? Someone else? It didn't matter. Moss put his foot on the accelerator, tried to outpace the vehicle, but the Commodore wasn't up to the challenge. The police cruiser closed the gap.

'Oh Jesus, oh shit, we've got to get away from him.' Hannah's eyes were wide, overflowed with panic.

'Hannah, calm down.'

Moss switched his gaze from the rear-view mirror to the road ahead. A two-lane stretch of black top, no visible side roads, no way to outrun Erskine, nowhere to escape.

'You don't fucking understand,' she said breathlessly. 'You don't know what he's like, what he can do. If he gets hold of me— '

The police car drew up on Moss's side. Erskine smiled over the barrel of his pistol, aimed at the front tyre, fired. Hannah's scream merged with the sound of exploding rubber.

Moss felt himself lose control of the vehicle. The police car slowed to get clear of the swerving Commodore, but not quickly enough, ploughed into it.

The police car rolled before his own vehicle plunged into a deep gully running along the side of the road. The jagged ground reared up at them. The windscreen exploded, showering Moss and

Hannah in broken glass. His head hit the steering wheel. A burst of pain exploded along his right leg.

He had no idea how long he'd been out. He was aware of blood running down his face from where his forehead had connected with the steering wheel. His leg throbbed; no blood visible, but probably broken. Thick brush poked through the hole where the windshield had been.

The passenger seat was empty except for Hannah's purse and the broken glass. The glove box hung open, the contents scatted on the floor. It took Moss a moment to register the gun was gone.

He thought he was going to pass out as he hauled himself out of the car, wiped the blood from his eyes with his forearm, heard something, a voice. He took a deep breath, gritted his teeth against the pain as he dragged himself up the slope towards the road.

The voice became louder. Moss recognised it – Erskine. He summoned all his remaining strength, pulled himself out of the gully, tried not to use the damaged leg, sat on the roadside.

The police car lay on its roof. Tiny shards of glass littered the bitumen around it. Erskine was half out of the side window, straining against something holding him in place, one arm outstretched, his face covered in blood. Hannah stood over him, the Smith & Wesson in her hand, oblivious to Moss.

'Hannah, help me,' pleaded Erskine. 'Come on, we've had some good times, some real good times.'

Hannah raised the pistol.

'For fuck's sake, girl, don't play around with that. It's fucking dangerous. Come on, I'll give you whatever— '

The shot silenced Erskine mid-sentence. The sound, like a whip crack, echoed in the trees. She fired again. Erskine's limp body jumped at the impact.

Hannah wheeled around, suddenly aware of Moss, locked eyes with him. Her white top was spotted with blood from a cut on her cheek. She shook her head to move a strand of hair that had fallen across her face. Her eyes narrowed as she gripped the weapon in both hands, looked down the barrel at him, held the pose, the pistol quivering in her hands.

Moss reached a hand out towards her. 'Hannah … no.'

She lowered the weapon, dropped it on the ground.

Moss realised he'd been holding his breath, exhaled deeply. The pain in his leg, which lay at an odd angle in front of him, was worse.

She walked past him, climbed down into the gully, and retrieved something from the front passenger seat. It was the shoulder purse.

Moss watched in silence as Hannah opened the purse, took out the postcard. Reassured it was there, she dropped it back into the purse, fished her jacket out of the back of the car, put it on and slipped the purse over her shoulder.

She climbed out of the gully, stood on the roadside next to him, looked at him, no recognition in her eyes, started walking.

Moss went to say something but stopped himself, watched her until she rounded the bend, disappeared from view.

He had an idea where she was headed. She had a long way to go.

Swimming Pool Girls

Melanie Napthine

It was school holidays so they'd placed an inflatable obstacle course in the middle of the pool. You lined up at the shallow end and, in pairs, raced the course, which took you climbing up the plastic steps of the inflatable structure and sliding down the planed surface of the other side. Then you skidded towards the twin rope ladders that took you up another incline from which you jumped (or were pushed) into the deep end of the pool below. You'd line up and a staff member would stagger the pairs going through so that there was no great pile-on in the middle.

Cal whooped every time he set off, and again when he made the leap into the bright blue water. He was hyper that day, the kind of state he described as being 'turned up to eleven'. It was funny – the little kids' toes might grip the very edge of the pool but they wouldn't move till the attendant called *go*. It was like they thought they were still at school. Whereas we older kids had constantly to be told *wait* or *slow down*. Then when we went through, we'd nudge and kick each other, Cal and I, each trying to dislodge the other from the structure altogether. I got him once with a well-placed kick at the top of the first climb, made contact with his ribs, and he was hurt or tickled maybe and he fell right off into the blue water and came up swearing and grinning.

*

We hadn't come with Bec and Chloe and Hannah and Nat. It was just coincidence that we'd bumped into them there. I'd been at Cal's place and his mother had gotten sick of us playing WOW and anyway she was having some friends over so could we get out of her hair? Cal lives just a block from the pool so we grabbed towels and went, hopping barefoot over the boiling asphalt. I was already wearing boardies and Cal had dropped his daks right there in front of the computer and called to his mum to chuck him a pair of bathers. He took the shorts from her without looking up from the screen – he was pissed off about being kicked out. He didn't wait for her to leave the room before wriggling into them, one-handed, still sitting, his other hand on the mouse.

*

At the pool, Cal looked around and made a splashy dive. He came up with his hair slicked down the back of his neck then grabbed me by the shoulder and tried to climb on my back. His sour breath warmed my ear, his untrimmed nails made half-moon scratches on my skin. I slid out from beneath his pinioning legs and dunked him, and we chased each other round the pool for a while. There were mostly younger kids on the obstacle course then and we swam clear of it for a bit. But then a kid about eight or nine years old leapt from the top platform right on top of Cal. Cal whipped round like he'd been attacked and the kid sort of froze, bobbing in the water. Then Cal made a fake grrr-face at her and flicked her with water and the kid squealed like she'd been showered with lollies and swam quickly away, grinning back over her shoulder at us like she wanted to be chased.

I said, 'Let's have a go on that thing.'

Cal ducked his head under the surface and came up shaking the water from his ears like a dog before saying, 'Okay.'

*

We were lining up for our third go when the girls arrived. I nudged Cal.

'Look who's just walked in.' Cal squinted. 'Hannah and them.'

Cal looked. 'Oi, Hannah,' he called, before I had a chance to.

Hannah swivelled towards the voice. She was in the middle of sliding out of her little skirt, one leg raised so that she made a hop as she turned. On her top half she wore a stringy pink piece of fabric tied high at her neck. Her stomach was the colour of cinnamon and there was a winking ring in her navel. The other three were looking too. Hannah gave a little wave and Bec was smiling. She had one of those enthusiastic grins that lift right up like a puppet's pulled by strings.

They took their time getting their gear off. Cal and I stayed in line but we were watching. Cal said, not quietly, 'Check that out,' when Chloe peeled off her t-shirt. His eyes had that glazed sheen they got when he looked up from a long gaming session. The girls sauntered over as though they owned the place. By this time Cal and I were almost at the front of the queue for the obstacle course.

'Come here,' he beckoned to them, and the girls squeezed in line in front of a couple of real littlies who backed up for them, big-eyed. Cal's damp thigh knocked against the head of one toddler, who wobbled but didn't fall. The child's mouth moved as though it might howl, but Cal glanced down with his glittering eyes and the mouth shut.

'What are you two doing here?' Nat asked. Nat may not have been as look-at-me as the others but she was slyer. She spoke in a little voice that made you lean forward to hear her properly, and you'd catch her looking at you sometimes, quick little glances like fish darting in water, so you were never quite sure if that gleam at the corner of your eye was what you thought it was. Right then, for instance, I saw her eyes go to Cal's ripped honey-coloured stomach, though she'd been addressing me.

'Something to do. Cal's mum kicked us out.'

Cal called her a name under his breath and Hannah's gaze flicked uncertainly between him and me. But Nat was leaning in close to hear him and Bec laughed her split-mouth laugh.

Cal and I let the girls go first, for the view.

'Two each,' Cal whispered to me, digging an elbow into my ribs.

They were tentative at first, still dry, but they got into it soon enough, squealing and yelping like puppies. One time Chloe and Nat were in front of us and I couldn't resist – I reached out and gave Chloe a little push, and Cal caught on and charged up behind Nat and then the girls were scrambling and squeaking up the climb and we chased and all four of us wound up tumbling into the first plastic valley in a mess of limbs and warm wet skin.

'Hey,' the attendant called after us, and a kid cried out, 'They're pushing in!', but we didn't look back. Falling into the water at the end I knocked my head against someone's knee or elbow and came up spluttering, dizzy, joyous.

Cal leant his head to one side and tapped the other to dislodge water. A strand of his long hair brushed Bec's shoulder, pale and beaded with water. Under the surface her creamy stomach undulated with the movement of the water. A little lip of skin overhung her bikini bottoms like a handle. She was generously built, Bec, in a way that made you want to grab a handful of that smooth flesh and knead it like dough.

*

The six of us treaded water for a while, just chatting, kicking each other sometimes under the water as we kept ourselves afloat, holding on to the edge of the pool. Hannah was telling us about some party on the weekend, which we faked having heard about, when a barrel-shaped object ducked beneath us and swam through our pedalling legs. It surfaced against the near wall: a kid with two dripping plaits, the one who'd earlier jumped on Cal's back. She was grinning slyly, looking at Cal. He said something to her that I couldn't hear and she climbed away up the ladder, keeping her grin on.

'Who's that?' Nat wanted to know.

'I don't know.'

'Let's go lie outside and dry off,' suggested Chloe suddenly, and we filed out, tippytoeing over the hot concrete. There was a triangle of grass there, startlingly green after the fogged air inside, and we laid out towels and dropped onto our bellies to let the sun swallow the diamonds of moisture from our backs. I was next to Chloe, which was fine with me. Cal was keeping close to Hannah. We talked for a while about school: who was going to be in whose class that year, what subjects we were choosing. This was the first year we really had options, which meant the beginning of the gradual closing down of possibilities that signified *growing up*. I didn't know what I wanted to be but if I took Maths instead of Geog, I'd never be a cartographer; if I stayed with German I'd never get a job translating in Tokyo with the robots and the sexy silent geisha girls. Bec had it sorted – she was going to be an accountant like her dad. Hannah thought maybe fashion but you need Maths apparently and she was in the vegie class. And then gradually the sun made us dreamy and still, and conversation trailed off like the wispy ends of the clouds that relieved the great sheet of blue sky over us.

*

'I could just fall asleep here,' Chloe murmured into her towel. I made a receptive noise, my eyes fixed on a dip in her lower back that looked felty and touchable as the underside of a sheepskin, lined with tiny pale hairs that shone gold where the sun got them. It led like a slide to the top of her bikini bottoms. Following the thin top seam of them round to the hidden front of her led to a dead end where her tidy stomach disappeared into her towel. There was a small gathering of skin, like a thread pulled in silk, at the back of her thighs. My finger ached to iron it out.

Bec really had fallen asleep, to tell by the deep sough of her breathing. Cal was telling Hannah some story about the time he and Ed got into Chasers with fake IDs. Hannah gave a soft chuckle, like air escaping a punctured tyre. Encouraged, Cal reached out splayed fingers and ran them up and down her back. She squirmed and rolled over, and took a hold of his hair. Then they were both wrestling and Hannah tumbled backwards onto my shoulder. She was hot from the sun, damp-haired still. She said *Oof* and *Sor-ry* but she was smiling and she dug her elbow into my chest to right herself. Hannah had a neat little smile, very tidy teeth like baby teeth, but her face was round and her features little and lost in the middle of it.

Cal said, 'You're ticklish,' as though he'd discovered the g-spot.

'I'm hungry,' said Nat suddenly. She might have been ignored but Hannah rolled over onto her side and said, 'Me too.'

Cal's hand slid from her back. The muscles in his cheeks were pulled tight. When I shook out the change that had been wrapped in my towel and said, 'Let's go to the machine,' he looked like he might protest. His lower lip twitched, but Hannah was already standing up. He glanced up at her standing over him, tying her towel around her waist, and then closed his eyes a beat longer than a blink.

Back inside, we bought chips and chocolate bars and Cokes. A little kid at the machine was counting out five-cent pieces in his hand, cross-eyed with concentration.

'Oh, cute!' Chloe murmured, and I opened my palm over the kid's and dropped a dollar. He looked at the coin as though it might evaporate in his hand, then closed his fist tight over it and looked around for someone to share his luck with. He didn't say thank you.

'Little shit,' murmured Cal.

'Oh, don't say that,' Hannah protested. Cal made a face that told her she was soft but he shut up.

He sat himself down on the edge of the pool and popped open his bag of chips. We all joined him, dropping our legs into the cool water. Hannah tipped her head to drop Smarties down her throat, catching them like a seagull catches chips. It became a game – Cal and her tossing chips and chocolates into each other's mouths, missing as many as they caught. A yellow one dropped – the water stained like someone had taken a leak. A red one – like someone had dipped a cut finger.

Of course, five minutes later an attendant made a beeline for us. A guy in his twenties maybe, bunched-up ponytail, whistle, pool t-shirt. He advanced with one hand palm out, as though he were soothing animals.

'Guys. Guys, you'll have to move. You can't eat over the pool.'

Bec giggled. Sitting down, her midsection rippled into a series of tubes like layer cake.

'Why not? There's no rule,' Cal said. He pointed at the board on the side of the wall that outlined the code of conduct. No running, pushing, divebombing. No mention of food.

'Yeah, but you're getting food in the pool. It's unhygienic.'

'No more than kids pissing in it,' I pointed out.

Chloe wrinkled her Pekinese nose. Hannah had a hand to her mouth, whether she was laughing or embarrassed or choking on a Smartie I couldn't tell.

'Yeah, well you'll have to move.' Then, conciliatory: 'You can come back when you've finished eating.'

'We're not hurting anyone.'

'Come on.' Hannah to Cal, standing up.

'You're getting food in the water. That spreads germs.' There was something endearing about the dogged way the guy tried to make us understand. He gestured to the Smarties sinking slowly in the pool, leaking dye like the tails of tropical fish.

'That's what chlorine's for,' persisted Cal. His cheeks were pink from the sun, the whites of his eyes scribbled in red. I half-rose, squatting balanced on the balls of my feet. This kid was only earnest, a joke but a mild one not worth milking, and I was concerned about the ripple of unease I sensed from the girls.

'Let's go,' I told Cal.

Cal swung his legs out of the pool and stood up. 'What the fuck is the chlorine *for* then?' he asked pleasantly. And he spat into the pool.

Hannah made a sound. I straightened and followed Cal outside. I heard Nat whisper something sharp to Hannah but the girls followed too. The sun blinded me momentarily; I stepped right onto Chloe's towel to leave a big damp footprint.

'Well, that was embarrassing,' murmured Nat.

'We're leaving now.' Hannah was folding her towel neatly, matching corner to corner. Chloe was slipping on a shirt; for a moment she was headless – two shortish legs with a long gold torso atop. Then gone, under cover of her Ponies t-shirt. I collapsed on my own towel.

'Got everything?' Bec made sure of the rest. Then, 'Bye Cal. See you, Seb. See you at school maybe. Bye.' And they left.

Cal called out, 'Tuesday,' presumably to Hannah, and bent to examine a toenail.

'Maybe we should head home too.'

But Cal turned his inflamed eyes away from me and stood up. 'I'm going back on that thing,' he said and I could do nothing but follow him back into the dim humidity of inside.

I half-thought we might be stopped by one of the pool attendants but they were both occupied; the girls' departure had not made an appreciable difference to the size of the crowd. We took our place in line. Cal held it poised on the rubbery balls of his feet, rocking slightly so that the fine erect hairs on his shoulder tickled my own. When we made the front he hardly waited for me, or to be told *go*. I clambered after him and slipped around like an idiot on the frictionless incline. Going up the rope ladder, Cal swung a leg out and accidentally kicked me. I lost purchase and fell into the water. My nose was flooded, I came up snorting and gasping for breath. Cal hadn't noticed. Charging to the finish, I saw him leap into the air at the end and I blinked the water out of my eyes at the same moment so that I saw on the inside of my eyelids the wild still shape he made, arms high, legs split, suspended in the air the second before he dropped. I made my way to him.

He was treading water and the kid in plaits was there again. She was feinting towards him, going under and then surfacing at his back, flipping herself about to do it again. I thought at first that Cal hadn't noticed her but then suddenly he turned when she was behind him and made a grab for her middle. He hoisted her up high and tipped her back into the water. She screeched like a stiff gate and her plaits strapped her face as she was upended. She bobbed up, face tight with surprise, but she spat out water and flung an unbalanced arm around Cal's neck to right herself.

'What are you doing?' he was asking her as I swam up beside him.

'Throw me in again,' she instructed.

He unpeeled her fingers from his neck. 'No.'

'O-oh,' she moaned, as though in pain. 'Please. One more time.'

'Who are you here with?'

'No-one. I've got no-one to play with. Katie was here, my friend Katie, but she had to go home.'

'How did you get here then?'

'My mum dropped me off.'

Cal squinted up at the roof. The girl paddled on the spot, waiting. Cal extended an arm in a quick blur of movement and tickled her armpit. She squirmed and laughed in a winded way.

'Hey, you coming back on?' I asked him.

He glanced at me blankly. 'Yeah. In a minute.' There was an odd note of relief in his tone, as though I'd arrived to spell him from an obscure labour. I turned back for the inflatable.

I went through twice on my own, each time hitting the water with a hard splash that caused a mother with a toddler by the benches to start with disapproval and draw her child close. I couldn't see Cal anywhere, though the place was so full of bodies it would have been easy to miss him. The kid was there, or I saw her rump at least, packed into bather bottoms with red and white stars over them. She had a bullet-shaped body, thick torso, with skin white as paper and dimpled from the chlorine. Her stomach pouched over the hem of her bathers in a tidy mound like an upturned crème caramel. One cheek of her bathers was hitched up. I watched her slide a finger beneath to hitch it down with the unselfconsciousness of the under-ten, then disappear into the toilets.

*

I sat by the edge of the pool for a while, scanning for Cal. He wasn't outside; the glass-plated sliding doors showed a bare patch of grass, though I could see a small scrap of colour in the green and wondered if one of the girls had dropped a hair tie. I watched the toddlers in the baby pool for a while. The water in there was kept warmer and a haze of hot air lay suspended above it, giving a sheen to the faces of the parents and their tiny ones.

The ache that had gripped me was gone. I felt as drained and empty as though I'd actually satisfied it. I was ready for home but first I had to find Cal. I walked the length of the pool and back, then made for the bathroom.

There was an old guy in there, towelling between his legs. There was no-one in the showers, no-one checking their hair in front of the mirrors. The toilets were reached through another door. Beyond it I could hear the sound of water running and a muffled laughter, as though through a hand over the mouth. The door groaned on opening and I was met with a sudden stillness. The prior sounds hung like shadows in the air; a stall door seemed just to have clicked closed. I waited: shuffling, a breath.

Only one of the stall doors was locked. 'Cal?'

There was a scuffle of feet, a 'ssh'. Then a clear, high voice said, 'We're hiding!'

'Yeah, well. Found you.'

Silence.

'You coming out?'

'In a minute.' Only Cal's feet showed at the base of the door.

I stood undecided for a moment, then opened the other door. 'See you out there.'

'Yeah.'

I opened the door but it closed itself. The old man had gone, leaving a trail of talcum footprints.

I went back on the inflatable. Nothing else to do, but I was getting tired of it by then and it was far less fun without the others. Now and then I glanced over towards the bathrooms but Cal didn't emerge; nor did the girl. I wanted to get home but I'd left my things at Cal's. So I waited some more, and finally he did come out, probably only fifteen minutes or so later, though it felt longer. The girl wasn't with him. I wasn't going to ask. He wasn't pale, wasn't flushed, not agitated or distressed. Ask me if I noticed anything and I'll tell you there was nothing *to* notice. When they found the girl the next day, I was as shocked as anyone.

'Let's go,' I told him and he didn't argue. We grabbed our towels.

Death Star

Tony Birch

Around fifty years earlier the town fathers had voted to plant an Avenue of Honour, a sentry of ghost gums stretching for a mile out of town on both sides of the highway. Each sapling represented the life of a soldier who had been lost in war. The trees grew tall and strong. No one at the time could have predicted that these monuments marking life would be the cause of more deaths, with trees drawing speeding cars and the bodies of young men driving them like moths to the flame. At the halfway point of the line of commemoration the greatest gum tree of all sat strong and squat on a bend on the highway, opposite the front gate of Telford's dairy.

Dominic Cross would often ride his pushbike out to the tree. He'd rest the bike against the trunk, climb into the trees lower branches and place his open palm against a deep scar that continued to bleed thick sap from a wound. He would think about his older brother, Pat, who'd come off the highway behind the wheel of a stolen car. Old Telford, heading back to his farmhouse after morning of milking had heard a car gunning along the highway, way off in the distance. As the roar came closer and rang deeper he turned and watched in awe as the car left the iced bitumen and glided through the morning mist with more grace than it should have had. The car slammed into the tree side-on and wrapped itself around the trunk. Telford was afraid to go near the car, certain that whoever was trapped inside was dead. He ran on to the farmhouse and telephoned the police. Later that morning he stood on his front verandah nursing a mug of tea and watched the mangled body of the driver being cut from the wreck.

Dominic hid from the world on the day of his brother's funeral. His mother had laid out a black suit and clean shoes for him the night before. When he failed to answer the knock at his bedroom door she opened it and found the bed empty. The suit was where she'd left it, draped over a chair by the open window. She searched the house and his father went looking for Dominic in the back garden and lean-to garage on the side of the house. The boy was nowhere to be found and his parents had no choice but to leave for the church in the mourning car without him. It was either that or be late for their eldest son's funeral. Dominic hadn't hidden in the house or the yard. He'd climbed the back fence in the early light and run along the track beside the creek. He didn't stop running until he'd reached the old cannery where he and Pat had spent most of their spare time when they were younger, a pair of trickers on BMX bikes, racing the length of the loading dock and leaping into thin air.

The news of Dominic's disappearance spread throughout the wake, held at the local football club changing rooms after the funeral. Ty Carter, who'd ridden with Pat, being a hot-wire specialist, volunteered to a worried Mrs Cross to track down her son. Ty knew where to look. He'd punished his own bike around the cannery when he was a kid and had helped Pat build a ramp off the end of the loading bay. He left the football club and walked to the cannery, half-pissed. He spotted Dominic before he'd climbed through a gap in the fence leading into the cannery. Dominic was sitting on the loading bay dangling his feet over the edge. He heard Ty coming, looked across to him, lay back on the rough concrete and looked up at the sky.

Ty tried climbing onto the loading dock and fell backwards onto his arse.

'Whoa.' He laughed. 'I'm fucked. Too many beers. What are you doing here, Dom? Your old girl is worried sick over you and the old man is gonna give you a belting. I reckon they're thinking you might have killed yourself or something. Why didn't you front for the service? He's your brother.'

Dominic rested his hands behind his head. 'Cause I didn't want to.'

Ty finally managed to haul himself onto the dock. He sat down next to Dom and brushed dirt from the elbows of his cheap suit. 'Fair enough. My older brother, Frank, when he died I never wanted to go to the funeral. They made me go, my folks. Wish I fucken hadn't.'

Dominic flipped over onto his stomach. 'Why not?'

'He'd been in the water for three days before they found him by dragging a long net along the river. Scooped him out like some rotten old king carp. He was fucked up. His face and the rest of him. The yabbies had got him. Should have screwed the lid of his coffin down. But my mum, she spoke with the priest and they kept the coffin open at the church. Funeral parlour put some makeup on him, puttied the holes and all. Didn't help. I didn't want to look at him. She grabbed me by the hand, tore me out of the bench I was sitting on and dragged me up the front to where the coffin was in front of the altar. Fuck. I could hardly recognise him. Looked like some monster.'

Dominic coughed. 'Was Pat's coffin open?'

'Nah. Thank god. He was too…'

'Mangled up?'

'Yeah.'

Ty didn't think Dominic was too upset about his brother's death, but it was hard to tell. The Cross boys had always been known for their toughness and didn't give much away when it came to emotional stuff.

'He was driving an expensive car,' said Dominic. 'Where'd he get hold of it?'

'Out at the country club. The tourists have been coming up here since it opened, for the golf and the pokies. Fucken golf. Me and Pat have been up there chasing cars most Saturday nights. They're hard buggers to wire, the new cars. Full of computer shit and all. I can get around it, but it takes time. I would have been in the car with him Sunday morning except my old man ordered me drive across to the west with him on Saturday night. We was supposed to be on a cattle run. Didn't find a single cow and come home with a pair of fucken goats. He slaughtered them Sunday morning and fed them to the pig dogs.'

'Who were you two working for?' Dom asked.

Ty was desperate for another drink. 'Haul down to the bottle-shop with me and I'll tell you about it. The work.'

Ty bought himself a bottle of whisky, staggered across to the playground opposite and sat on a rusted swing. He unscrewed the bottle and threw the cap at a sign riddled with bullet holes: *Tidy Town – 1978.*

'You know Georgie Barron who runs the scrap yard?' asked Ty.

'Sure. He used to run stock cars at the drag track. Dad used to take me and Pat there on a Saturday night.'

Ty took a long swig from the whiskey bottle, like a man in the desert dying of thirst. 'About six months back we were out there at the scrap yard, Pat and me, going through the wrecks after a sports wheel for my Commodore. I could hardly believe it when we found one. We pulled it out with the tools, walked over to George's hut by the gate and ask *how much for this?* I couldn't believe it when he said we could have the wheel for nothing, and any parts we wanted to strip off the wreck. It would have been a great deal but there was a catch.'

'Like what?' Dom asked.

'Like if we could find him George a Nissan SS. *Like fuck*, I told him. There's nobody in town who drives an SS.'

Ty took another drink out of the bottle and looked across to the empty highway.

'So, what happened?' Dom prodded him.

'The shifty bugger was a step ahead of us. He told us that some fella had been coming up to the country club from the city most weekends for the golf and a wrestle in the cot with some woman he was having an affair with. *He drives a beautiful red SS, George said. You get me that car and we're in business, boys.* The info on the car was spot on. Around three the next Sunday morning me and

Pat watched the car from the rise above the club. It was dead quiet, we strolled down to the carpark and were out of there within five minutes, Pat screaming his lungs out behind the wheel of the car soon as we hit the highway.'

'Why'd he want you stealing a flash car for spares? Makes no sense.'

'Nothing like that. George is married up to some Asian woman. They move the cars to someone who ships them overseas. We made good money out of the deal, me and Pat. Then three weeks ago we hit the jackpot. A two-door Merc. Almost brand new. Took me fifteen minutes to turn it over. Should have seen George's face when we drove it into the scrap yard. I thought he was gonna start pulling himself.'

'How much did you get for it?'

'Nothing. Not yet. They work with a dealer in the city. The wife runs the show and she don't pay until she has money in her own hand.'

'The boss?'

'Yep. She's frightening. Looks like some Kung Fu killer. We're overdue. Five thousand. Pat's half is yours, Dom.'

Dominic spat on the ground.

'Dunno that I want money. If Pat hadn't been stealing cars for them he'd still be alive.'

'Maybe. And maybe not. You know how Pat was. He'd lift a car for money. And he'd steal one just to wind the windows down and roar along the highway in the night. I'm gonna drive over to the yard tomorrow and ask where the money is. You want Pat's share or not?'

'Why'd you tell me? No-one would know if you kept it all.'

'I might be a thief, Dom. But I'm not a bastard. You in?

'Suppose so. Yeah. I want the money.'

George Barron's scrap yard sat at the dead-end of a mile-long stretch of gravel road. Ty borrowed his father's ute, telling the old man he'd picked up some landscaping work. He fishtailed along the road, leaving a snake of dust in his trail. George had inherited the scrap business from his father along with a decent bank balance. He rewarded his good luck by belting the piss day and night. It took him less than a year to run the business into the ground. Down to his last ten thousand dollars he took off to Asia for a sex holiday. His drinking mates at the Pioneer Hotel were surprised when he returned with a Filipino bride. George bragged to them that he'd bought himself a housemaid and bedwarmer. His new wife, Maxine, had other ideas. She was sharper than George. Maxine was also tough. Unknown to him, before meeting George she'd run a lucrative gambling house in downtown Manila. Maxine had never so much as picked up a broom and wasn't a woman for keeping house. Why she ever agreed to move to a rundown country town in Australia with the under-educated, boozed up and overweight George was anyone's guess. Maxine had a nose for business and soon had the scrap yard back on its feet. She quickly became known for her ability to bargain mechanics and motor hobbyists into the dirt. Once the yard was turning a dollar she turned her energy to the more lucrative stolen car racket and set up a partnership back home moving stolen luxury cars.

*

Ty and Dominic walked through an open gate into the scrap yard. Ty knocked at the open door of the shed that passed for the office. Dominic could see Maxine sitting behind a desk. She was smoking a thin cigar and shuffling a pack of playing cards. She dealt herself a hand of patience and looked up at Ty through the haze of smoke.

'What you want today, boy?'

'We're after George. Is he around?'

'George is in the toilet. You talk to me.'

Ty wasn't sure what to say. He was too afraid to ask her for the money. The toilet flushed and George appeared at a curtained doorway hitching up his pants.

'The kid is for you,' Maxine said, louder than she needed to. Ty felt a little insulted. He was no kid. He was turning nineteen next birthday.

'What are you doing here?' George asked, not bothering to buckle his belt.

'The money you owe me and … Pat. You haven't paid yet. For the Mercedes.'

'Pat.' George laughed. 'Fucked himself up good and proper. No coin heading his way. What would he spend it on?' He chuckled.

Dominic's feet shifted in the gravel. He didn't like George.

'Knock it off,' Ty said. 'This is Dom, Pat's little brother. I've been telling him about our deal with you. What was coming to Pat goes to him. I've explained it.'

Maxine dealt another row of cards, watching George out of the corner of one eye. He offered Dominic an open hand. 'I'm sorry about the business that went on with your brother. Pat was a good worker. I'm sorry to be losing him.' He turned to Ty. 'But I don't have any money for you. Not yet. We've had no luck moving the motor. I got it sitting under a tarp in the workshop out back. Might be able to get it on the next consignment. I've got a couple of beautiful cars back there.'

Ty was sure George was lying to him. 'But it's been three weeks.'

'If you don't fucken believe me I'll show you the car.'

'Why can't you pay now?' Ty pushed him. 'We done our work. You can get your money back when you sell it.'

Maxine had heard enough. She turned over a last card, stood up and walked around to the front of the desk. She waved a long manicured fingernail in front of Ty's face. He followed the nail like someone who'd been hypnotised.

'You boys. Last time you make mistake and bring the wrong car here. My customers don't want the colour. It is bad luck. I have to pay now to change colour. Very expensive. I get less money. You wait now and get less money too.'

'How much less is less?' Ty asked, speaking barely above a whisper, he was so intimidated.

She looked past Ty to Dominic. 'Five hundred. Each.'

'Five hundred! George, you promised us five thousand dollars for that car. You rubbed your hands together and jumped up and down screaming that it was *gold*. Those were your exact words. Fuck it. This isn't fair.'

'Hey!' George screamed. 'Don't you be swearing in front of my wife, son. Maxine's a Catholic.'

'But you promised,' Ty pleaded. 'Five thousand.'

'Don't matter what I said. You watch your mouth.'

Maxine stepped forward and ran the tip of her sharpened nail down Ty's left cheek.

'I tell you something, kid. I feel sorry for you and your friend who die. I give you two thousand dollars. And you bring one more car. Special car. And we double. Four thousand dollars. Other boy is dead now. You can make all the money for yourself.'

'It doesn't work that way,' Ty said, pointing at Dominic. 'Pat's cut goes to his younger brother.'

'Your business, not mine.' Maxine smiled. She pointed her finger to the ceiling. 'You bring one car more. We pay.'

The following Saturday, around midnight, Dominic was perched on a boulder overlooking the Country Club car park. Ty lay on his back in the damp grass enjoying his third joint of the night – on the back of the half-a-dozen beers he'd downed earlier in the evening, and a couple of unidentifiable blue tablets handed to him by Big Roscoe on the door of the *Motorhead*, a pokey shopfront that passed for the town's only nightclub.

Dominic surveyed a line of cars. They didn't have dent or cracked windscreen between them.

'Hey, Ty, where do you reckon they get all the money for these cars, the people from the city who come up here?'

'My guess would be that most of them are lawyers, coppers and crims.' He took a long drag on his joint and held the smoke deep in his lungs as long as he could before blowing it out. 'Drugs. It's where all the big money is. We deliver this second car maybe we could pool the earnings. Buy in some coke, in bulk. You imagine them on the gear around here. Go fucken mental on it.' He got to his knees, fell forward onto his face and began giggling like a child.

'You sure you're okay to drive, Ty?'

'I'm good to go. I always have a beer and weed before a job. Eases me into the work. Dunno why, but I can get nervous behind the wheel. You remember driver ed back at school, Dom? *Safety first.*' He giggled again. Ty gave up trying to get to his feet. He lay on his back and looked up at the clear night sky. The stars shone from one side of the dark blanket to the other. A full moon sat above the mountain range directly ahead of them. 'You doing any of that astronomy shit at school? Looking up at the sky?'

'Next year, if I'm still there. Mr Macleod takes a class out to the hills camping with this telescope he's got. It's like a cannon.'

'I know. I went one year with him. Me and Pat and some others. He ever talk to you about it? You know Pat was mad for the stars. His best subject at school.'

'He never mentioned it to me. Only thing Pat talked about was cars.'

Ty raised an arm in the air, extended a finger and waved it across the sky. 'Well, he liked the stars too. Can't steal them though. And he knew the names of every one of them … what do you call them? Clusters or something?'

'Constellations.'

'That's them. Fucken constellations.' Ty pointed to a particularly bright star low in the sky. 'You see that one?'

Ty was slurring his words. Dominic looked up at the sky, unsure which star Ty was pointing at. 'What about the star?'

'Well, the time Macleod took us camping he aimed his telescope at one of stars. I reckon it's that one. It's in the right place, anyway. He lined us up and got us to take a look at the star through the telescope.' Ty sat up and wiped his mouth, as if there was something very important he had to say. 'And you know what he told us?'

Dominic wasn't paying attention. All he could think was that Ty was in no state to hot-wire a car let alone drive it back to Barron's yard.

'You listening, Dom? You know what he told us?'

'No, I don't. What did he tell you?'

'I know this sounds crazy but the star we were looking at that night, the same star you can see up there winking at you now, it's dead, Dom. Fucken dead.'

'Dead?'

'Yep. And it's been dead for a million years. Maybe more than that. The light you can see up there, it's taken all that time to get here. Right now that star, where the light is coming from, I know this sounds like bullshit, it's already dead.'

Dominic looked up at the star, burning bright yellow at the centre with exploding red sparkles at its edge.

'It sounds like bullshit to me, Ty. A star as bright as that one, I don't see how it could ever die.'

He buried his hands in his pockets and began walking away.

'Where you going?' Ty screamed at him. 'We got this job to do. One car and we hit the jackpot. It's what she said.'

'You believe her, that she's gonna double your money?'

'I got no choice.'

'Well, I do.'

'We stealing a car or not?'

'Nup. I'm going.'

'You going home?'

'No, I'm not.'

'Where you off to then?'

Dominic kept walking. Ty stood up, dropped his pants and pissed in the dirt. By the time he'd finished Dominic was halfway across an open field behind the country club, taking a shortcut through the bush to the scrap yard. Ty ran after him, screaming, 'What about the car?'

*

An hour later Dominic sat in the bough of a tree on a hill a half-mile above the scrap yard. He was able to pick up the scent of petrol in the air. he looked up at a crimson sky, lit by a burning Mercedes two-door sedan. Ty lay at the base of the tree, sleeping like a baby, until the car suddenly exploded, shattering the windows of the row of cars parked beside it. One of them quickly caught fire. Then another. And another.

DEATH STAR

The Teardrop Tattoos

Angela Savage

You cringe when you see my tattooed tears. But driven by the same impulse that makes you slow when you pass a car crash, you look closer. One is transparent, a silhouette. The other, clear at the top and blue at the bottom, looks swollen, like it might roll down my cheek at any moment.

Who would do that to themselves?

I hear your mind ticking over, hear you whisper *gang, murder, prison.*

'Does it mean she killed somebody?' The boy is young and cocky, doesn't know to hold his tongue. His mother shushes him and steps up the pace. I want to yell out, 'Yeah, I did,' but his mother has dragged him away from the scary dyke and her dog. One of those dangerous breeds, she's thinking, the kind they train to fight.

I don't hate her. She's only doing her job. Protecting her boy.

People think I'm a lesbian because of the way I look, though I've never had sex with a woman, not even in my mind. I haven't had sex with anyone at all in a long time, but not even the tattooed tears are enough to put some men off trying. Sully scares away the last of them.

Sully is a dangerous breed, an American pit bull. I got him through a contact I made in the rat house. I read up on dogs – had fuck all else to do – and concluded an American pit bull was the one for me. They've got a bad reputation. They look mean. People give them a wide berth. But get them when they're young and train them properly and you can't go wrong. Loyal, intelligent, protective, loving. My husband had none of these qualities. I could bloody well have them in a dog.

The guy I got him from said Sully was blue. But to me he's the colour of storm clouds with a streak of white on his chest I think of as his silver lining. He lies on his back as I run my fingers up and down his white streak, gives me a black-lipped grin and pounds the floor so hard with his tail I worry the neighbours in the flat below will complain.

But Sully isn't just a defence. He's my friend. A dog's affection is still more than I deserve, but Sully doesn't hold that against me. The flat where we live is in Brunswick, one of those inner city Melbourne suburbs where wogs and yuppies collide. Not my choice, but beggars can't be choosers. At least I got a place where pets are allowed. I would've preferred a car. Me and Sully could've slept in it, taken off whenever we wanted, made a home of the open road.

But you can't check in with your parole officer when you're on the road.

The powers-that-be gave me a place three doors from a childcare centre. I can't hear the children if I keep the windows shut. Me and Sully try to stay out of sight at drop-off and pick-up times, though it means lying low for up to two hours at each end of the day, which isn't always possible.

It was winter when I moved in. The childcare centre opened at sparrow's fart and some kids were dropped off while it was still dark. Through the Venetian blind in my bedroom I watched mothers unbundle their babies from capsules and car seats, drawn faces illuminated by the interior lights of their SUVs. I watched them juggle their babies on one hip, close the car door with the other, stagger lopsidedly to the entrance and punch in the security code. When they reappeared minutes later, the women were light on their feet. I watched them dab at baby spew on lapels, slip into stilettos, touch up lipstick in rear-view mirrors.

I felt nothing for these women. Neutral as Switzerland, me.

When the childcare centre traffic died down, I'd take Sully to the park. Well, not so much a park as a grassy block surrounded by temporary fencing with a hole in it. It reeked of a failed development – like a builder had overcapitalised and didn't want to crystallise his losses by liquidating his assets. You surprised someone like me says things like *overcapitalised* and *liquidate assets*? Yeah, well, you would judge a book by its cover. Just so happens in a past life I was a girl from a nice family with a Diploma of Business and a promising career in insurance. Not that it matters now. No-one's ever going to give me a job in insurance.

One day, Sully and me ran around the park long enough to work up a sweat, even though it was only September and the sun wasn't quite strong enough to knock the chill out of the air. While I squeezed out through the hole in the fence, Sully ran ahead of me towards the flat and nearly collided with a woman coming down the hill pushing a pram.

Apart from a purple scarf, the woman was dressed head to toe in black. Her hair was black with purple streaks. The pram – the fancy kind that costs as much as a car – was also black and purple. She slowed as I neared in that way of mothers who expect you to ooh and *ah* over their kid. I only glanced at it. Four or five months maybe, wearing a hand-knitted beanie. And fuck me if the beanie wasn't black and purple too.

The woman smiled. No-one had fucking smiled at me since the night I killed my husband.

'Hello,' she said.

'Hello.'

I turned to make sure she could see my tattoos.

'Nice to see some sun.'

'Yeah.'

'Cute pup, What kind is it?'

'American pit bull.'

'Oh?'

She struggled to maintain her smile. But if looking like a murderous dyke wasn't enough to put her off, Sully was. I was enjoying my smug moment so much that I nearly let Sully scamper off the edge of the gutter and into the traffic. I scooped him up with my foot, dumped him on the footpath and smacked him hard across the face. American pit bulls have such a high pain threshold, I had to be forceful so he'd get the message not to run out on the street. Sully yelped in surprise and I saw the woman's smile take another hit as she added *animal cruelty* to the list of things she hated about me. She leaned into the pram and fussed over the kid's beanie.

'Well, me and Charlie better get going,' she said. 'See ya.'

She headed to the crèche at the bottom of the hill, trailing disapproval like a vapour in her wake.

When the letter came a week later, I knew who was behind it.

Council has received advice that you are in possession of a restricted breed dog, namely an American pit bull terrier, this being a breed whose importation into Australia is prohibited absolutely under the Commonwealth Customs (Prohibited Imports) Regulations 1956. As of 2 November 2005, the Domestic (Feral and Nuisance) Animals Act 1994 *makes it an offence to acquire a restricted breed dog...*

Shit, an offence would be a breach of my parole.

Council records show you have not registered your dog. All residents are required by law to register their dog by age three months. Persons applying to register their dog must make a declaration as to whether their dog is a restricted breed. A sizeable court penalty applies for a false declaration. Council cannot accept the registration of restricted breed dogs.

Fuck. I couldn't keep Sully without registering him, but if I tried to register him I'd get done for acquiring a restricted breed. So much for Sully's silver lining. Why the fuck couldn't that woman have left us alone? Why did she have to stop and talk to me? Couldn't she read the big neon sign over my head saying *Fuck off*? And why did I tell her what kind of dog he was? She'd wrong-footed me with her smile and her chit-chat about the weather. Now losing Sully was the price I'd pay for being fucking polite.

I stood a moment in the galley kitchen of my flat, holding the council letter, burning with rage. It was a slow burn, not a conflagration. I was in control. Then, a eureka moment. It almost made me wish I could attend another session just to tell the group about it.

'Check it out,' I spoke aloud, as if they were there in the kitchenette with me. 'Anger therapy's worked. I'm controlling my impulses. I'm going to take my time, really plan my revenge to be sure to hurt this woman like she's hurt me.'

Sully, the sweet little mite, thought I was talking to him and drummed the floor with his tail.

That night I took him back where I got him. I didn't think I had enough heart left to break, but saying goodbye to Sully proved me wrong.

*

My first step was to find out where she lived. It's not easy to observe someone undetected when you weigh nearly ninety kilos and have tattoos on your face. You can't march into a childcare centre and ask to see the records for 'Charlie'. Shit, I didn't even know if Charlie was a boy or a girl. Could be either these days. I was at the local video store when the solution came to me. A DVD called *Kiss Kiss, Bang Bang* caught my eye. A Val Kilmer movie I hadn't seen, though I saw a lot of his movies in the rat house. My favourite was *The Saint*, where he had all the gadgets and disguises. That's when it struck me: I could disguise myself. I might not have Val Kilmer's budget, but I had a Savers down the road and a Vinnies around the corner. Stuff was cheap at Savers and if I played my cards right, the old dears at the Vinnies might give me what I needed for free. My spirits lifted for the first time since losing Sully. I grabbed *Kiss Kiss, Bang Bang*, found *The Saint* and took both DVDs to the counter.

The video store guy caught me smiling. Nearly scared the shit out of him.

I spun a story to the two old dears at the Vinnies about being a single mum in hiding from a violent bastard who forcibly tattooed my face.

'I only want to buy my groceries—' I deliberately used the old-fashioned word '—without having to look over my shoulder.'

Well, fuck me if the old biddies didn't mobilise like a pair of retired army officers. One of them, Eunice, found me a couple of wigs: a grey curly one much like her own hair, and a long brown one with a thick fringe.

'We get them from cancer patients,' Eunice said. 'Survivors,' she added quickly, as if it mattered. 'They don't need the wigs once their hair grows back.'

While Eunice rifled through the racks, the other one, Carmela, put together an ensemble she called the Nonna look: black cardigan, shapeless black dress, black headscarf to go over the grey wig. She teamed this with some low-heeled, lace-up shoes and even found me an unopened packet of support stockings. Eunice reappeared with a blue tent dress, lambskin vest, beige boots and sunglasses with lenses the size of beer coasters.

I wasn't crazy about trying it all on but the old dears were keen and I wanted to keep them sweet. The Nonna look was brilliant. My own mother wouldn't have recognised me. If she did, she would've crossed the street, but that's beside the point.

'*Un momento*,' Carmela murmured at my reflection in the change-room mirror. She ducked off and returned with a black handbag. 'I think *le vedove* will try to speak *italiano* with you.'

'Vedovay?'

'The widows.'

She adjusted the lacy headscarf to hide the tattooed tears. 'Perfect.'

Eunice's hippy shit looked better than I'd imagined. It was years since I'd felt hair on my shoulders or worn a dress. I looked like one of those jovial plump women with an appetite for life, the type I normally did what I could to avoid. In the interest of authenticity, I let Eunice drape a string of beads over my head. But when she reached up to remove the sunglasses, I flinched.

'May I?'

A voice you'd use with a wounded animal.

I couldn't see what she was doing, felt something cool and damp press against my right cheekbone. She stepped back.

'Much better.'

I looked in the mirror. She had covered over my tears.

'Concealer.' She pressed a small cylinder into my hand. 'Hides a multitude of sins.'

I was too shocked to speak.

*

I used the Hippy Chick disguise to tail her. When she passed by my apartment window again, pushing her fancy pram, I gave her a twenty-second headstart, crossed the road and followed her up the hill.

Her house turned out to be a fifteen-minute walk in the direction of Sydney Road. If Brunswick was a body, Sydney Road was the spinal cord that held it all together and made it move. There's nothing suspicious about a hippy on Sydney Road, so I followed Pram Woman until she turned into the entrance of a sand-coloured weatherboard house opposite a small park.

At last, a lucky break. I slowed my pace and paused to rub an imaginary blister on my heel, used the park fence for balance. A row of spindly shrubs blocked my view of Pram Woman's house, but the front door was clearly visible through the gate in her picket fence. A tortoiseshell cat sprang out of the way as she pushed up onto the verandah. The number on her mailbox was 124.

Early next morning I walked down the same street in my Nonna disguise. A dark-green sedan I hadn't noticed the previous evening was parked out front. I headed for the park and chose the bench with the best view of the house. Someone had covered one arm of the park bench with a knitted sleeve. I'd seen fence railings, bicycle stands and signposts in the area clothed in random bits of knitting like this. Was it a joke? A message? Not knowing made me uneasy. I shuffled to the other end of the bench and took out a string of rosary beads I'd found in the Vinnies handbag. I'd long ago stopped believing in God, but I figured people would leave me alone if they thought I was praying.

Just before seven, a passing car projected a missile that hit the verandah of number 124 with the thud of paper on wood. The front door opened and the woman dashed out, snatched the newspaper, dashed back in again. Hair standing on end and wearing a too-tight black tracksuit, she made me think of a trapdoor spider.

Twenty minutes later a man in a suit appeared. Lean and polished, I could practically smell his aftershave from across the road. The green sedan beeped as he made for the driver's side, mobile phone against his ear before he'd even fastened his seatbelt. It was quiet for almost an hour after that. I sipped at a bottle of water and ignored the growling of my stomach.

A curly-haired woman with dark circles under her eyes entered the park behind a careening toddler. She sat on a swing and watched as the boy scooped up handfuls of tanbark and flung them into the breeze. I watched the boy, too, accidentally made eye contact with the woman. She gave me a tired smile. I had my hand on the beads in case she came over but was saved by the arrival of a second mother-and-child duo. They all seemed to know each other. I returned to my surveillance.

Around eight-thirty my target re-emerged in her trademark black and purple and turned her pram in the direction of the childcare centre. This time the baby wore pink – a girl then. As soon as they were out of sight, I crossed the road at a pace appropriate to an overweight and elderly woman and paused out front of the house as if to catch my breath. I hadn't heard the telltale beep of a burglar alarm and there was no sticker in the front window, no blue light on the roof. The left side gate was covered in vines, the right was a recycled wooden door left ajar.

No alarm, no dog, ample cover and a gate left open. This was what the burg' merchants in the slammer would call a 'dream job'.

I took a tissue from my handbag, wiped my nose and leaned over the front fence to use the bin. The recycling bin was closest. Amid the empty wine bottles, newspapers, tins and plastic I found what I was looking for. An envelope addressed to Belinda Hyatt.

I spent a week of mornings in the park, getting a handle on the daily routine. Hubby worked fulltime; Belinda did three days from home, the days little Charlie went off to childcare. When she had the baby with her, Belinda usually went out. Once I followed her to a café on Sydney Road. It was jammed with prams. A sticker on the window said, 'Breastfeeding welcome here'.

Sydney Road swarmed with old women in black. I'd barely noticed them before, but now that I was one of them I saw them everywhere. And I realised how much we had in common. Their public grief set them apart. My tattooed tears served the same purpose.

I learned to impersonate their rolling gait, a pace that allowed me to cruise past Belinda's house even when she was working. Through the shrubbery I watched her in the front room at her computer, the tortoiseshell cat lolling on her desk like an oversized paperweight.

I undertook evening surveillance in my hippy guise. You didn't see so many Nonnas out after dark, but as Hippy Chick I could always pretend to be going out or heading home, depending on the hour. Most evenings were quiet at Belinda's, the green sedan always home before seven. Lights shone from windows at the rear where the kitchen was located, moving later to the lounge room at the front. The place was dark by eleven.

I turned up one evening to find Belinda's husband in the front yard watering the garden. The baby was suspended against his chest in one of those carriers, arms and legs flapping like a pull-string puppet. The man was chatting to the baby but paused as I walked past to give me a straight-toothed smile that made my eyes water. I kept walking until I found myself outside a pub on Sydney Road.

The barman's pierced eyebrow made him look permanently surprised but he didn't blink when Hippy Chick ordered a pot. The smell was room deodoriser that reminded me of prison, so I headed out to the beer garden. It was like walking in on a summer camp. A pack of hairy men played ping-pong, exchanging banter with the young women at a nearby table who were drinking beer and knitting.

A guy at a table on his own was smoking rollies and reading a book. I thought next time I should bring a book too, then laughed at myself for imagining there would be a next time. One of the hairy guys approached me. I almost told him to fuck off when I realised he was only after the ping-pong ball that had rolled under my table.

'Thanks.' He smiled. I smiled back. He went back to his ping-pong game. I wiped the sweat from my upper lip. A couple walked in, tattooed sleeves interlinked. On their heels was a Staffie, blue like Sully. I looked at the empty space at my feet. If it wasn't for

Belinda, Sully would've been there too, making me smile with his goofy grin and thumping tail.

I drained my beer and left.

The following night it was after twelve when I ventured onto Belinda's property. It was dark apart from a dull glow in the second window on the right side – a night-light in the baby's room. I inspected the window: old wood, new lock, key dangling in it. Jemmying it open with a crowbar would be easy but noisy. I made my way to the back of the house.

The yard was organised into garden beds, a fig tree on one side, lemon on the other. A small deck held a trestle table and chairs. Security door, more key-locked windows... Belinda and her hubby weren't as slack about security as I thought.

A flash of light caught my eye. I took a closer look at what was on the table. Leadlight. A work in progress. Perhaps a feature window or a panel for the door. Leadlight was an activity we were offered in the rat house as an alternative to boredom, until the screws twigged that Traci 'The Fox' Ferrigno was using the classes to conduct her own lessons in the art of glass cutting for B&E purposes.

I scanned the yard again, registered the shed in the corner. It was wide open. On a low shelf were Belinda's leadlight tools: pliers, rulers, brushes and glass cutters.

A square of light came on.

It beamed into the yard from the house. Someone was stirring. I crouched in the shadows by the shed, then hurried back the way I'd come.

Sounds from the baby's room. I squatted beneath the window and listened. Floorboards creaked rhythmically, a muted female voice accompanying the gentle drumming. I thought Belinda might be pacing the room, though I hadn't heard the baby cry. Then recognition hit me like a punch in the guts.

Belinda was in a rocking chair with Charlie at her breast. I just knew it. I slumped to the ground, my back pressed against the weatherboards, my tears like acid.

*

The right night presented itself a week later. New moon, north wind, wheelie bins out front. I wore black jeans, a long-sleeved t-shirt and sneakers; carried a Swiss Army knife in one pocket, WD40 in the other.

Not a night for disguises.

I reached number 124 at four a.m., the quiet time between the baby's one o'clock feed and the man's six-thirty jog. I let myself around the back and took the glass cutters from the shed. The rusty wire screen on the window tore like tissue paper and the wind masked the sound as I carved a hole in the glass large enough to insert my hand and disengage the widow lock. A squirt of WD40 enabled me to ease the window open with barely a sound. I'd learned well from Traci The Fox.

My heart speeded up as I prepared to teach Belinda Hyatt how it felt to lose what she loved. I scooped up the warm body at the end of the cot, held closed her mouth and nose, hauled her back out through the window with me and slashed her throat with my knife.

The body jerked in spasms for a few moments then flopped in my arms, silent and still. I stood fixed to the spot, blood seeping into my clothes, the weight growing heavier in my arms. I expected to feel excited at this point, even elated. Instead, I was appalled, even as I felt compelled to see my ghastly plan through.

I retraced my steps to the front of the house and arranged the body on the door step where it would be seen when Belinda emerged to collect the newspaper. My hands were sticky with blood and even in the dim light I could see black liquid pooling on the doormat.

I stepped back, taking in the bloody tableau, trying to imagine Belinda's reaction. The horror in her face. The likelihood she would scream. But still I felt no satisfaction. Only disgust.

But I was a hardened criminal, for fuck's sake. I had the teardrop tattoos to prove it.

Then it was as if the characters I'd been playing had gotten under my skin: the tetchy old Nonna who commanded respect; the Hippy Chick with so few cares in the world that she probably knitted covers for street posts. I'd spent the past few weeks blending into a community. A door had opened that I'd believed was closed to me forever. Could I step through it? Or should I bolt it shut for good?

I returned my gaze to the mess on the doorstep. My Nonna thought about cleaning it up, burying the body in the park or disposing of it in a wheelie bin. Hippy Chick dreaded the thought of Belinda coming to the door with Charlie on her hip. But I reckoned the baby was too young to get upset at the sight of a dead cat.

Besides, I was only going through with this for Charlie's sake. Belinda needed to know her house was not secure. She needed to do more to protect little Charlie. The dead cat would be a wake-up call.

A wake-up call.

Would it have saved my baby if I'd called home from work that night? He might not have heard the phone through his drunken stupor. But perhaps the sound would have roused my son before he could suffocate in his sleep.

The transparent tear, that's for my lost baby. The other tear is for my husband, who put the baby to sleep on his stomach. My mistake was killing the bastard. I did it to punish him, but all it did was release him from the terrible pain I lived with every day. Grief so profound, so permanent, not even tattooed tears can do it justice.

I needed to put distance between me and the cat. I jogged back to my apartment, bagged my bloodied clothes, showered and dressed again to add the bag to the wheelie bin. When I turned to go back inside I spied something in my mailbox. Another letter from the council. I ripped it open and read by the foyer light.

Council wishes to advise that we found no evidence to substantiate the claim that you are in possession of a restricted breed dog. Consequently, the childcare centre has now withdrawn its complaint on this matter and you are no longer under investigation.

I caught my reflection in the plate-glass door as it closed behind me. You see my teardrop tattoos?

Look closer.

The Good Butler

Carmel Bird

So mum, do you think this is really Nicole?

Nicole who?

Nicole Kidman.

Hmm, I'm not sure.

Or is it someone made up to look like her?

Or is it her made up to look like someone made up to look like her?

Caroline is the mum and Daisy is the daughter. Caroline has terminal cancer, and she's got about six months to live. Perhaps a year, they say. She reads a lot of magazines. Daisy is showing her an advertisement where a glamorous woman in a deep red satin dress is stiffly posed on what could be a bed in a motel, staring into the camera half crossly, with a half-smile and half-sneer, as if she is thinking, *Get on with it, you idiot.* Or does she look a bit scared? It's hard to tell really. She certainly looks uncomfortable, whoever she is. She has long blondish movie-star hair, groomed and falling over her shoulders. Long arms and hands, knobbly knuckles. Probably a wedding ring. High-high-heeled shoes, coffee-coloured, lie carelessly on the carpet in the foreground. One leg dangling over the edge of the bed, stockings containing her toes in a little silken sack. And the shadow of her foot points to a message.

Look at what is says, Mum. This is hilarious. It's an ad for Etihad Airlines. You don't just travel First Class, you travel in a thing called 'The Residence'.

Listen:

The Residence

Three room retreat. Separate living room. Ensuite shower room. Double bedroom. Personal butler. Flying Reimagined.

Caroline took the magazine from Daisy and read what it said. Her only comment was: 'No hyphens. I wonder why they don't do the hyphens? Is it a thing now?'

'My god, this wouldn't just cost an arm and a leg, they would have to take your heart and your liver as well. Kidneys too,' said Daisy.

But Caroline had fallen asleep.

Daisy closed the magazine, added it to the pile of others on the broad table beside the bed, smoothed her mother's rug, patted the pillows, patted her hands, kissed her lightly and left the room, taking the tray on which the tea had gone cold in the silver teapot, and where the delicate cress sandwiches lay almost untouched on the delicate green plate. A small white vase of pastel poppies, petals crushed, folded, hairy pods open wide. Wide.

Daisy sat in the nearby sunroom, looking out across the tops of two old apple trees that were busy with white blossom, blushing pink. She knew there were bees. Caroline would never see another spring. Daisy had a pot of coffee and a croissant. Her iPhone was charging on the table in front of her. Whenever Caroline needed her she would send her a text. When she was a child with chicken pox she used to have a little brass bell from India beside her bed, and she could summon her mother or her father to her bedside. Her brother, Dan, got jealous and hid the bell in the garden where it turned up years later none the worse for wear.

She opened the newspaper and read:

'Flight attendant union calls for UN women's ambassador Nicole Kidman to stop endorsing Etihad Airways over claims its practices are discriminatory towards female staff.'

So it *was* Nicole in the picture. That cleared that up.

But the main news story was about the Germanwings A320. The picture on the front page showed a crumpled fragment of the plane. The jagged piece of metal bore a clear print of the German flag, bold bright black, red and yellow stripes. The whole thing resembled a battered cigarette packet, lying on a harsh grey slope. Dust.

'The pilot at the controls of a Germanwings jet that crashed in the French Alps accelerated the plane into the mountainside, killing all 150 people on board, according to French investigators,' she read.

Caroline was only dozing, drifting in and out of thought and memory and daydream. She had heard what Daisy said about selling your body to pay for The Residence. It would be more apt to sell your house. Then you could reside in the little air-borne house in the clouds. With the butler. The butler? Was that a title and a euphemism? Would he attend to your *every* need? Did sexual preferences apply? Or perhaps he could procure for you from a wardrobe or refrigerator of gorgeous lovers. All tastes catered for, all things re-imagined. The butler did it. The butler made up to look like someone made up to look like the butler.

Her mind had become strangely fertile in recent weeks. It operated with a startling clarity, but moved into realms before unknown, or untapped. As her body faded, her imagination flourished. She had moved beyond fear into a weirdly manageable world of relentless fantasy. She even realised that this was 'a stage' of 'the process', and she made a decision to stay in the stage. They told her 'life is a journey', but in her private conversation with them, the conversation they never heard, she said 'death is a journey'. And there were staging posts. She was going to remain forever in the stage of brilliantly-lit imagination. It was strange that Etihad spoke of 're-imagining' even though they couldn't quite get the hyphen. Caroline had always loved punctuation. The name 'Etihad' sounded like some sort of medication. Ten milligrams of Etihad with food.

She opened another magazine. There was the Nicole figure again. The interior of The Residence seemed to resemble a somewhat dreary motel in a grungy suburb of Sydney. Of course, the butler would make a big difference. She turned a few pages and found a story about a house in New York that had been sold for one hundred million American dollars. Was she reading straight? Yes, one hundred million. Good grief! Now if you sold that you could fly round in The Residence for quite a while. Not that she knew how much The Residence would really cost. By a curious coincidence, the New York house was called The Residence also. Like on *Sesame Street*, it must be the Word of the Day.

Caroline owned her house, the house where she was going to die, leaving the tea cold in the silver teapot – her husband had died some years before. She imagined selling the house, which was probably worth about one million Australian dollars, and taking off in the flying motel that was The Residence. With Jeeves, a lady's gentleman. They talked about a 'bucket list'. She had said she didn't have one. Maybe she did. Maybe she could sell the house and go for a ride in The Residence. Then she really did fall asleep.

When she woke up, Daisy took her out into the sitting-room where they watched *The Antiques Roadshow.*

'Look, that teapot is almost exactly like mine,' Caroline said.

And indeed it was.

'Eight hundred pounds!'

Then they watched the News, and the leading story was about the airbus near Seyne-les-Alpes. An image taken from a helicopter – a leaden grey ravine in the base of which lay another fragment of the aircraft, this one resembling a crumpled dark red handbag.

'Imagine if that had been the Nicole Kidman plane, instead of a cheap German one,' Caroline said.

'Well it wouldn't have made any difference.'

'No, of course not. I just meant that the person in The Residence and their butler, with all their Mouton Rothschild Pauillac 1982, could easily end up as a squish of DNA in the French Alps.'

And that is how the idea took hold. Caroline had always been a bit of the gambler by nature. A punctuator and a gambler. Other things besides of course, but they are probably irrelevant here.

In her bright imagination stage, she would lie in bed devising simple – oh, it was all so simple – plans to sell the house and buy a flight in The Residence on the chance that the pilot would fly into a mountain. The End. Did she spare a thought for the other passengers who would be unlikely to be intent on death by suicide-pilot? Actually, after the first excitement of the plan, she did.

Naturally, she wasn't silly enough to put any of this to Daisy – Daisy and her brother were supposed to be inheriting the house. How could she be so unkind as to deprive them? She seemed able to brush this thought aside. And gradually the second plan took hold of her. Not a gamble on having a suicide pilot. No. It was this: she would sell the house, pack her bags, take The Residence to somewhere and quickly make her way to Switzerland or Mexico or wherever she could find a good service from Doctor Death. Or perhaps, even better, perhaps the Residential butler was in fact the answer. A good butler, yes, a good butler will do whatever you ask. Oh this was a bucket list and a half. She smiled a lot, and sometimes laughed aloud at the delicious fruits of her imagination. Re-imagining her imagination. 'Mum passed away in The Residence,' they would say. It was sad. It was for the best. She would smile and laugh. Sleep. She recalled the old TV advertisements about AIDS – the Grim Reaper comes forward out of a swirl of eerie clouds, he cuts the family down. All fall down. Horrible. But now the Good Butler. The Good Butler. He comes with the goblet of Mouton Rothschild, and there is quiet chamber music soft and quiet and pale velvet cushions and the soft perfume of honey in the sunlight and the coo coo coo of a lonely dove and a goblet of Sèvres crystal sparkle and glitter and here comes the butler and he offers the best cocktail ever ever, in the second goblet, and you lie back on the Residential motel blanket – quiet pointed stockinged feet tiptoe, dark red dress, closed eyes, long blond hair, hair fresh from a blow dry – blow kiss and sip – and kiss and sip – and you sip and you sip – and you drift and I drift – and I sip and I drift – and the poppies shiver in the shade and the sun – and apple blossom clouds go sailing by – and by – and I sail by and by – and bye-bye bye-bye.

Bye.

The Drover

Leigh Redhead

Scott Tallis stood at the whiteboard, attempting to write through the pain. It felt like a nest of fire ants had taken up residence in his skull and were biting into the backs of his eyeballs. When he got to the end of the sentence his trembling hand dropped the marker and he staggered as he bent to retrieve it. He covered the blunder with a comedic reel across the front of the classroom.

'Bloody loose carpet,' he muttered.

Nobody laughed. The class stared at him with their characteristic look of stupefied boredom. Beads of sweat formed on his upper lip and the tang of gin wafted out from the pores of his skin. He glanced at the clock above the board: 10.51am. *Jesus Christ*, he thought, *I've only been in the room six minutes.* The prospect of another ninety-four (it was a double period) almost made him sob. He would have called in sick, but had been unable to come up with a day's worth of covers at 7am. Besides, he was a new teacher and if he put a foot wrong he wouldn't make it to the end of his six-month probation.

I've just got to get through today. Just today.

*

Scott had been invited to the writers' festival for the first time in years, to speak on a panel with his old friend Phillip Docker, and

Dawn Holland, an up-and-coming author who shared the same publisher. Phil had taken up most of the talk time and all of the questions, but that was understandable – he'd recently won the fifty-thousand-dollar Watson and Moore prize for his war novel, *The Drover*, so he was the undisputed star of the show. His signing queue had stretched all the way out of the book shop and down Flinders Street. After the event Scott and his wife Natalie, Phil, Dawn and their publicist, Sophie, had retired to the Gin Palace, one of the subterranean Melbourne bars that had so delighted Scott when he'd moved from Adelaide all those years ago. The lighting was low, the furniture baroque and Dean Martin crooned from the speakers. For the first martini, things had been fine. Scott remembered Phil leaning across the table and clapping him on the shoulder.

'It's great to see you, mate,' Phil had said. 'And again, congrats on the new baby. Must have your work cut out for you. Should I ask how the writing's going?'

'No.'

'Still working on, what was it? Something historical?'

Scott nodded. 'Set in eighteen sixty-nine. Reams of research, a huge, sprawling mess. I've got over six hundred thousand words. Of crap.' He looked at Sophie. 'I guess I shouldn't be telling you this. I've already spent the advance.'

She looked clueless for a second. 'Oh, are you still under contract with Wet Ink? Sorry – I didn't know.'

'Difficult second novel?' Phil chewed his olive with teeth that were a lot whiter than Scott remembered, spat the pip discreetly into his napkin. 'Tell me about it. Remember *Cargo*? Sold about five hundred copies, most of which were at my book launch. Sunk without a trace.' He spoke with the good cheer of a man whose third novel had been subject to a much-publicised bidding war.

'*Cargo* was a great book,' Sophie said. 'It just didn't get the attention it deserved.'

'Thanks, but you're paid to say that. It was shit.'

Scott remembered when the book had been released and the small, mean thrill he'd felt when it had been savaged by a reviewer in *The Age*.

'I was reaching for the stars with that one.' Phil sighed. 'But I just didn't get there. Do you ever?' He looked at Scott. 'The gap between what we want to accomplish, and what we end up with… Still, I think I got a little closer with *Drover*.'

All the women were nodding. Natalie had her hand on her chin.

'Closer?' said Sophie. 'Phillip, you nailed it. Everyone agrees.'

Phil looked down and waved the praise away.

'Great to see you doing so well,' Scott coughed. It felt like a piece of olive had wedged in his throat. 'Gives the rest of us hope.'

'You'll get there,' said Phil. 'Hey, got a copy of *Drover*?'

Scott pulled the novel out of his satchel and Phil signed the title page and held it out for Scott to read.

Dear Scott,
Remember – you are not given the desire to do something without the ability to achieve it.
Best, Phillip Docker

Scott smiled tightly. Nice of Phil to acknowledge his talent, but the quote read like a fitness centre poster or a self-help slogan. *If you can dream it, you can do it.*

'Working at the moment?' Phil asked.

'He's teaching.' Natalie said.

'Writing?'

'No, high school,' said Scott. 'The Bayside Academy?'

Phil, from Sydney, shrugged.

'Ooh, hoity-toity,' said Dawn, dressed in what could best be described as goth-meets-Kate-Bush. Her flaming curls and pale, cantilevered bosom – along with her novel's many erotic scenes – had seen her plastered on the cover of the arts insert of all the major dailies. Scott would have bet money she'd attended a private school herself.

'What do you teach?' Phil asked.

'English.'

'How long?'

'Nearly six months. Finished the Dip. Ed. last year. Got a job in term two.'

'We really needed the money.' Natalie slugged back the rest of her martini and held up a hand to order another. Scott followed suit. The gin burned pleasantly as it trickled down his esophagus, the warmth expanding into his chest.

'I've been the sole breadwinner for the last five years; now it's his turn. Gives me time to concentrate on motherhood and my art.'

*

Scott looked up at what he'd written on the board.

Lennie Smalls is really big and retarded and this is an unsubtle metaphor for the pathetic helplessness of the working class in America. Steinbeck gives him no more humanity than a drover's dog in order to make his big stupid moral point.

His upper lip trembled as he read the words. He had no memory of writing them. He wasn't going to make it: his eyes felt dry as rusted ball bearings, his brain couldn't construct a coherent sentence and he could barely stand. Time for plan B.

'Actually, ladies and gentlemen, what might be better for you today is to have a look at some key scenes from the film,' he said and the usual half-hearted cheer went up.

He rummaged in his bag. *Oh, god, please let it be in here.* When his hand registered the smooth case of the DVD he ripped it from his satchel. Then he saw the title, *Entourage Season 7.* The pressure in his head extended into his gums and it felt as though his teeth might shoot out like popping corn.

*

'You're a sculptress, right?' Phil asked Natalie.

The women started laughing, throwing back their heads and exposing their throats. Scott could see Sophie's back teeth and Dawn's epiglottis.

'What did I say?' Phil widened his eyes.

'*Sexist,*' said Natalie, batting him on the shoulder. 'It's sculptor.'

'Oh. I'm sorry, I'd no idea.' He grinned wickedly so they would be in no doubt he was lying.

Natalie was sitting very close to Phil on the velvet love seat. She'd kicked off her shoes, tucked her feet under her legs and was practically snuggling in. Dawn leaned over the table towards Phil, breasts threatening to spill out of her corset, and Sophie fingered the stem of her martini glass. Scott noticed his teeth had started to grind, and excused himself to go to the bathroom. He urinated, washed his hands, and squinted to examine himself in the mirror. He'd gone casual: old jeans; converse shoes; checked shirt over a band t-shirt, but now wondered if he just looked pathetic – trying to seem younger than he was. He was thirty-seven, still had a head of thick brown hair, but his boyish look had evaporated after the baby arrived, sleepless nights cutting crow's feet into the corners of his eyes. Still, he was better looking than Phil, who, to be honest, looked closer to fifty than forty and had a kind of bulbous nose.

*

A voice piped up from the back of the classroom. 'You alright sir? Looking a bit green.'

Scott didn't have to glance up from his bag to know who was taunting him – Hamish Thorsten, white-blond, arrogant son of a QC. Hamish ruled 11B.

'Head cold,' Scott said.

Hamish whispered something to his offsider, no-necked, Rugby-playing Lachlan Farr-Baden, whose 'Haw-haw-haw' set the rest of the classroom giggling.

Normally, Scott would have asked Hamish to share his observation with everyone, if it was so amusing, but he was desperate to put on the DVD and turn out the lights.

'Settle down, everyone. Slight change of plans. Instead of the film, we're going to watch a related text that highlights some of the major themes in the novel such as the emptiness of the American Dream, the importance of friendship in a cruel world and the loneliness of the working man,' Scott improvised furiously. 'It's called *Entourage* and is about a Hollywood actor who—'

The class burst into excited chatter.

'Oh, my god, Adrian Grenier is so hot. I'd totally do him!' screeched Ophelia Howard, the resident valley girl. Her best friend, Ali, a bookish brunette, laughed so hard she nearly fell off her chair.

Scott saw Lachlan turn to Hamish. Under the general classroom babble, Scott caught the words 'sluts' and 'tits'.

'Lachlan!' Scott shouted.

'He was just telling me it's a brilliant show,' Hamish said. 'Lots of actresses with their, um, assets revealed. You rock, sir.'

The mocking tone made Scott want to wrap his hands around the kid's neck.

'It's quite a bit more than that I can assure you. Alright, pens out while I cue it up.'

'Can I take notes on my iPad?' Hamish asked.

'No.'

'But I'm a kinaesthetic learner. My educational psychologist says I need the new technology because I struggle with traditional learning methods. It's in my file.'

Scott was about to tell him to piss off, until he remembered the stack of shrinks' reports he'd been given on the first day.

'Sure, fine,' he acquiesced. He finally got the DVD playing and in the semi-darkness buried his face in his hands, gingerly probing the dimensions of his hangover.

*

When he got back to the table his third martini had arrived and he took a large swig before munching through both olives. He hadn't eaten since breakfast. Amazingly, they were all still praising Phil's book. Scott had read it – you were sent the other panellists' books for free – and could admit it was solid, if also a bit more commercial than his previous work. There was a real sentimental streak, obviously designed to appeal to the female demographic, but hey, they were the ones who bought books, right? Good on him for playing the market. Scott wasn't jealous – he knew he was the better writer – but he wouldn't have minded just a fraction of Phil's money to get them out of the hole they were in. Natalie had insisted on buying a place (in Brunswick!) and although her parents had helped with the deposit the monthly repayments were breathtaking.

'I'm simply a storyteller…' Phil was telling the women, but Scott didn't think that was why they were hanging on to his every word. Success had settled about Phil like a patina of fairy dust, bringing instant charisma and sleeker looks. Even the globular nose seemed less offensive, kind of Roman and heroic.

'How much did you actually make on the book deal?' Scott blurted. 'Was it really more than a mill?'

'I don't like to talk about money,' Phil replied.

'How about Dawn's book?' Sophie quickly changed the subject. 'I thought it was really beautiful, so accomplished for a first novel.'

'Wonderfully lyrical,' Phil said, and Scott wished he'd got in first. Lyrical was what you said when a book didn't have any discernible plot. The waiter came and took orders. Phil, soft-cock that he was, ordered a Perrier.

Scott switched to Shiraz.

'What did you think?' Dawn asked Scott.

'Honestly?'

'Of course.'

'It was certainly poetic. You have a deft touch.' Where was he getting this shit? 'But I had a bit of a problem with the inner life of your male character.'

'Gabriel?'

'I'm not sure you quite nailed him.'

Dawn's mouth became a thin, hard line.

'Don't get offended.'

'I'm not offended.'

'He was kind of like a chick in drag.'

*

'Mr Tallis, are you asleep?' a voice bellowed as the lights snapped on, and Scott nearly leapt out of his chair. Clearly, he'd drifted off, but for how long? Lewis Brayfield, his teaching mentor and head of the English department, loomed over him, nostrils quivering.

'Of course not, Lewis. Just, ah, thinking for a second.'

On the TV screen a pair of young women were giving the lead character an exceptionally thorough lap dance. Scott scrambled for the remote control and stabbed at the buttons, hitting pause just before the bustier of the two completely removed her bikini top.

Lewis tugged his waistcoat down over his rotund abdomen.

'Can anyone here explain to me what this has to do with John Steinbeck?'

Lewis had had it in for him ever since he'd shown Scott the unpublished manuscript he'd been working on for twenty years. How was Scott to know he'd be offended by constructive criticism?

'Well, it's about the nature of the American Dream and how it…' Scott faltered, his feverish brain refusing to join the dots. Lewis looked triumphant. Scott tried to moisten his mouth to speak, but his tongue was sandpaper. All of 11B were looking from him to Lewis, except for Hamish, who gazed at Scott steadily, the corner of his mouth lifting into a smirk.

Ophelia wiggled in her chair. 'Ooh, I know this, Mr Brayfield!'

Scott shook his head and willed her to shut up.

'It's about sex!' she announced. The girls looked at each other and rolled their eyes and the boys grunted like warthogs. 'No, I'm serious. Like … what's his name from the book?' She nudged Ali. 'His wife's a total ho…'

'Curly?' Ali offered.

Lewis turned to Scott with raised eyebrows.

The silence was interrupted by a soft cough. A student in the front row had raised his hand. Somboon Aksornpan, aka Sammy.

'Yes?' Lewis called on him. Scott didn't have enough saliva even for that.

Sammy stood and clasped his hands in front of him. '*Entourage* is a visual text that portrays the emptiness of the American Dream. Its emphasis on material wellbeing and physical decadence demonstrates the spiritual impoverishment of the characters, and juxtaposes the modern-day version of the Dream with its initial conception, exemplified in George and Lennie's simple pastoral ideal.' He gave an almost imperceptible bow and sat back down.

Scott stared at the boy, slack jawed.

Lewis coughed into his fist. 'Of course, of course. You're absolutely right. Very good, carry on.'

*

Natalie shook her head at Scott and turned her attention back to Phil. Well, two could play at that game. Scott shifted his leg so that it rested lightly against Sophie's thigh. She didn't move away. There had always been a subtle attraction between them. Ever since his first book, the reasonably successful dirty realist novel *The Street*, had (jointly with Phil) won the National Young Writer's award. Luckily for Phil, a writer was still considered young at thirty-five.

'Chick?' Dawn raised her eyebrows and opened her red-lipsticked mouth.

'No, no. Hear me out,' Scott said, aware that he was waving his hands around more than usual. 'He didn't quite ring true. His inner life, thoughts and feelings seemed…' he took a big gulp of Shiraz and groped for the right words, '…filtered through a young, naïve female lens. I'm sure young women will really like the character, because he a mirrors them, but that's not how a man thinks.'

'Do you agree?' Dawn turned to Phil.

'No, I think Scott's being unfair. Gabriel was a sensitive character, sure. But I found him very relatable.'

Relatable?

Dawn smirked triumphantly as Phillip went on.

'Gabriel may not have been tough enough for Hemingway here, but I have to say I saw certain aspects of myself in him.'

Scott snorted and took another large sip of wine. A little dribbled onto his chin but he managed to wipe it with the back of his hand before anyone noticed. Sophie shifted in her seat so they were no longer touching. Natalie started to drone on to Phillip about her upcoming exhibition at the community centre and Dawn got out her iPhone and began to furiously peck at the screen. Scott's wine was nearly finished, so he motioned to the waiter for another.

*

Scott shot Sammy a grateful look, switched the DVD back on and turned off the lights. Walking back to his desk he noticed Hamish and Lachlan huddled over the iPad, sniggering, so absorbed that they didn't notice him inching his way around the perimeter of the room. With a fast, soft-shoe shuffle and a final unsteady leap, Scott was behind them, peering over the boys' shoulders at what seemed to be a wide-eyed woman fellating a horse.

There was a burst of movement as hands flew over the screen and the image was quickly replaced with a few typed sentences. Scott seized the device, Hamish grabbed the other end and they tugged.

'Hey!' Hamish protested. 'That's my property. Let go!'

'You dirty little pig,' Scott grunted, suddenly winning the battle and staggering back with the iPad.

'Mr Tallis!'

Jesus, it was Lewis again. Hovering in the doorway with his comb-over and his tweed.

'What on earth is going on here?'

'He's touching my personal property!'

'This … student,' Scott said, swiping at the iPad, 'was looking at hardcore pornography during class.'

'Sir, I was just taking notes. Mr Tallis is lying.'

'You little bast—'

'*Mr Tallis*,' Lewis boomed. 'Would you step outside?'

*

'So, how long you in Melbourne for?'

Scott rested his arm against the back of Sophie's chair. His leg touched hers again, softly, as though by accident. While Natalie was dark and cultivated a bit of a gypsy look, Sophie was sleek, with blond hair tied back in a bun, subtle beige makeup, and a slick of shiny gloss over full lips. She was staring into the middle distance, taking a long time to answer.

'Sophie?' he prompted, nudging her thigh. Abruptly she stood up, clutching her handbag.

'Could you please stop touching me? It's making me very uncomfortable.' She dashed to the bathroom.

He looked around at the others. 'I wasn't—'

Dawn glanced up from her furious texting. 'You know, I suspected you were a misogynist when I read your book. All those degrading sex scenes.'

'They weren't… What are you doing?' He looked at her phone.

'I'm quoting you on Twitter. Chick in drag. Young naïve female. And then you grope our publicist.' She lifted the phone and snapped a picture of him before continuing to type. 'Hashtag ScottTallis, misogyny, literarysexism.'

A shadow fell across the desk and Sammy looked up. Hamish had obviously grown bored without his iPad and was looming over him, the freckled, red-haired gorilla Lachlan by his side. Mr Tallis and Mr Brayfield were still not back and Sammy covered the book he was reading with his forearms.

'Way to suck up to Tallis, bum-boy,' Hamish said.

Sammy squinted up at them. 'What?'

'Ooh,' mimicked Lachlan. '*Entourage* juxtaposes the American dream of blah blah blah. Let me suck your dick, Sir.'

'Are you *reading*?' Hamish said *reading* like someone else might say *wanking*.

'No,' said Sammy, instinctively sliding the book closer to his body.

Hamish got that dangerous, sideways smile. 'Give us a look.' He held out his hand.

Sammy shook his head and they were on him in a flash: Lachlan behind, yanking his elbows, and Hamish in front, trying to wrest the paperback from his weakening hands.

'Hey,' Ali shouted as she and Ophelia marched over.

'Leave him alone, cockheads.' Ophelia crossed her arms and tossed her hair.

'Shut up, *I'll-Feel-Ya*,' Hamish said, pulling the book from Sammy's grasp and stepping back to examine it.

Ali punched Lachlan on the shoulder and the rugby player let Sammy go with a laugh. 'Love the S and M, babe.'

The other students sniggered. Hamish's sneer grew broader as he turned the book over and read the back cover.

'You fucking prick,' he said softly. 'I've got you now.'

'What?' Lachlan danced around him, trying to see.

'Where'd you get this?' Hamish asked Sammy. 'Tallis give it to you?'

'No, I bought it in an op shop.'

'Give him the book back.' Ophelia said. 'You're already in enough trouble over the porn.'

'They won't find any porn,' said Hamish.

*

'Hey.' Scott reached for Dawn's phone. He wasn't on Twitter, but he knew what a hashtag was. Before he could grab it Phillip stood up and laid his hand on Scott's shoulder.

'Time to get a taxi, mate.'

'Don't call me mate,' Scott rose up and shook him off. 'The salt-of-the-earth Aussie persona doesn't really gel with the Hugo Boss jacket. What are you worth now? It's more than a million, right?'

'You should leave.'

'I'm so sorry,' Natalie said to Dawn. 'He's not used to drinking this much, after the baby. So good to see you.' She hugged Phil and kissed his cheek.

'Stop fucking touching him!' Scott seized her bicep and for a second it looked like Phil was going to put up his dukes like an old-fashioned boxer, but Natalie ran up the stairs and Scott followed. Outside in the cobbled laneway a light rain misted the evening air.

'How dare you embarrass me in front of those people?' Natalie hissed. 'My first night out in over a year.'

'You were all over him. What are you now, a star fucker?'

'We need to get a cab and you need to sober up. You've got school tomorrow.'

'Fuck school. I'm getting another drink.'

*

'I know what I saw,' Scott said.

They had not found any porn on the iPad. Nor had the school IT tech.

'Yes, well, there's nothing we can do without proof.' Lewis looked relieved. 'I suggest you give the device back and apologise to the boy.'

Scott was going to do no such thing. He took a detour past the staffroom and hid the iPad in his pigeonhole, under a pile of marking.

Back in the classroom there had been a minor miracle. The students were quiet. Doing homework, messaging each other, shopping for shoes on their phones. Hamish Thorsten was *reading*. He looked up from his book when Scott walked in.

'Excuse me sir,' the boy drawled, 'may I have my iPad back?'

'Sorry Thorsten. IT has sent it off for forensic testing. Can't say how long...'

Suck on that, dipshit, he thought, headache dissipating slightly. He had never seen Hamish read anything that wasn't on a screen, and couldn't help asking what it was.

'*The Street*,' Hamish replied, turning the book over to read the jacket blurb. '*The dirty realism of Tallis' snovel is supported by the saltiness of his language and the startlingly erotic nature of his imagery. You can smell the soiled bed sheets and feel the sting of the needle hitting the vein.'*

The rest of the class looked over.

'This is my favourite part, Sir,' Hamish started reading out loud. '*Rosie's sex had come up in a bumpy red rash, like the skin of a freshly plucked chicken. The sharp black stubble stung Victor as he thrust his—*'

Scott hurried across the room and grabbed the book off him.

Hamish and Lachlan looked at each other. Lachlan burst into a fit of braying giggles, sucking in air like he'd punctured a lung.

Hamish sniggered softly, 'What's the matter?'

'That's not appropriate.'

'But you wrote it, Sir.'

Students gasped and craned their necks to see the cover.

'It doesn't matter who wrote it. James Joyce could have written it. But you don't use language like that in class.'

'I don't understand. I can read it, but I can't speak it aloud? That doesn't make sense.'

'Outside, Thorsten. *Now.*'

Once Hamish had joined him in the corridor, Scott closed the door. He didn't say anything for a while, just looked him up and down. He resembled a poster boy for the Hitler youth: platinum hair, pale blue eyes, and that bored, heavy-lidded expression most of the boys sported.

Scott moved close, glad he had a couple of inches over the kid.

'Try another stunt like that and you'll be sorry.'

'Sir?'

Scott leaned into Hamish's face. 'Piss me off again, and I will seriously fuck your shit up. Understand?'

Scott was gratified to see Hamish's eyes widen, just for a second.

'You can't talk to me like that. I'll—'

'Whinge to your parents? Get Daddy to call a crisis meeting like you did when I gave you a B+? I don't care, Thorsten. Now get your stuff and go see your Head of House. I've had enough.'

*

Scott pushed through the rusting gate and staggered up the overgrown front path, found his keys (yes!), dropped his keys (fuck!), picked them up and stabbed them at the lock until finally he was in, bouncing from one side of the entry hall to the other. *Hey Honey, I'm home! No. Quiet. Don't wake the baby. Never wake the baby.* He turned the knob to their bedroom door with exaggerated care. The bed was neatly made, cot empty. A note on the kitchen bench said that Natalie had taken the baby and gone to stay at her mother's. Scott opened the fridge. A litre of organic milk sat next to a long-neck of Cooper's Pale.

Just what he needed. A cleansing ale.

*

The rest of the lesson passed uneventfully and when the students left Scott had a merciful free period before lunch. Unable to deal with the staffroom, he decided to stay where he was, guzzling from his water bottle and surfing the net. He opened his email, hoping for a reply to the apology he'd sent Natalie, but she hadn't responded. There was, however, a message from his old uni friend Dan, who had been trying (and failing) to get published for years.

Dude, you should check out Twitter – you are totally trending!
#ScottTallis #Misogyny #Literary Sexism.

Scott pinched the bridge of his nose. Twitter. Honestly. Who was even on that stupid site apart from celebrities and the sad social misfits who trolled them? He deleted the message and another popped up in its place, this one from Wet Ink Press. He felt a momentary thrill – a movie option? International rights? But it was his commissioning editor, telling him that his contract had been cancelled for non-delivery of manuscript. Scott doubted that was the real reason, but before he could hit reply there was a knock on the door. He turned. Bloody Lewis, this time with a security guard in tow and – holy shit – was that the Vice Principal? The three of them walked across the room, shoulder to shoulder like the cast of a low-rent cop show. Hamish Thorsten. Had to be. Too late, Scott remembered that Lewis was Senior School Head of House.

'I'm going to need you to step away from the computer,' Lewis said.

'Excuse me?'

'Just do it,' said the Vice.

The security guard gave Scott an apologetic look, closed the laptop, unplugged it from the wall and placed it in a bag made of clear, thick plastic which he sealed with tape.

'What's going on?'

'We've had a student complaint,' said the Vice, who looked like the bad guy from a Dickens novel. 'Pornography.'

'*Entourage?*' Scott was confused.

Lewis cleared his throat. 'It's been alleged that while you were out of the room a student used your computer to look something up on the internet.'

'But they're not allowed—'

'And while doing so encountered images of a lewd nature.'

'That's bull—'

'Images of female students,' hissed the Vice.

'*Lewis*,' Scott implored. 'You know as well as I do that Hamish Thorsten is trying to get back at me for confiscating his iPad.'

'I can't disclose the complainant's name.'

The Vice pulled himself up to his full height and put on his assembly voice. 'The Bayside Academy has a duty of care and legal requirement to thoroughly investigate allegations of this nature, and report such incidents to Victoria Police. As outlined in our policies and procedures document, you are to be suspended with pay while the investigation is carried out. The guard and Mr Brayfield will accompany you to your office to collect your things.'

'This is ridiculous,' Scott said. 'They won't find any porn on my computer because there isn't any. That sociopath is stitching me up.'

'If that's the case then you've nothing to worry about,' said Brayfield. 'The truth will out!'

Scott started laughing then. A high-pitched keening that caused Brayfield and the Vice to share a long, worried look.

In the office Scott swept his mug, stapler, and *How to Survive Your First Year of Teaching* into a small copypaper box. He cleared out his pigeonhole and handed Hamish's iPad to Lewis. Giving the room a final, visual sweep he noticed a familiar book on Lewis's desk.

'*The Drover.*'

'Magnificent. Just magnificent,' Brayfield nodded. 'Did you know it's on the Year Twelve syllabus next year? I saw Phillip Docker speak at Readings last week and got myself a signed copy. Told him I was writing a book myself and he was very generous with his advice.'

Scott picked up the book and opened the dust jacket to inspect the title page.

To Lewis,
You are not given the desire to do something without the ability to achieve it.
Best, Phillip Docker

Scott had to pass through the staffroom to get to the carpark. He mumbled goodbye, but none of the other teachers looked up from their cup-o-noodles. Outside it was cold and clear, pale sunshine highlighting the sandstone walls, oak leaves budding green against a deep blue sky. A new building was being constructed over by the football field and for the first time Scott noticed the sign. *Coming soon: The James Thorsten Aquatic Centre.*

Scott unlocked the door to his 2002 Holden Barina and chucked the box on the passenger seat. As he started up he saw a flash of navy and turned to see Hamish and Lachlan saunter past, fists shoved in blazer pockets.

'Check out the shitbox,' Lachlan said.

'I'd be embarrassed to – oh – hi, Sir,' said Hamish. 'Nice car.'

'I know what you did,' Scott said quietly.

'Sir?'

'And when they examine my laptop and find nothing you're going to be in a lot of trouble.'

'Sure it's clean?' Lachlan asked. 'You're always ducking out of class, leaving it open. And those naked selfies everyone's sharing. Ophelia, Ali, and don't forget the younger girls. Year nine are the worst!'

Lachlan laughed. 'True, dat!'

'I know my own computer,' Scott said.

'The desktop, sure. But what's hiding deep in the system files?'

Hamish and Lachlan slouched towards a P-plated BMW convertible.

*

'Aren't you worried?' Lachlan asked as they approached Hamish's car. 'I mean, they can work out to the second when a file's been downloaded. Trace its origin. You can go to jail for that shit.'

'Chillax, I didn't touch his computer. Just wanted to make him sweat.'

Lachlan high-fived his friend.

*

Scott pulled out of his spot, then reversed into a three-point turn. The boys were shooting the shit, leaning on Hamish's hundred-thousand-dollar car. It occurred to Scott that despite everything, he had done it, he had somehow *got through today*. Traffic was light this early in the afternoon, so he'd be home in forty minutes. Oh god, how he wanted to be home: lolling on the couch, Tom Waits on the stereo, ice-cold beer in hand. He put the car in drive and was about to accelerate when he heard his phone beep. He braked and fished it from his jacket pocket. A message from Natalie. Finally!

Hi Scott. I think we should take a break for a while. I'm going to stay in the house so I'd like you to be out by the time I get back tonight.

Scott's head throbbed and vision blurred. His tongue tasted bitter, as though his salivary glands were oozing poison. In front of him, directly across the carpark, Hamish tilted his head back and laughed, flaxen hair gleaming in the sun. He looked at Scott and smiled.

The Barina *was* a shitbox, but it could still do zero to sixty in ten seconds. As he eased his foot off the brake, he wondered what sound a body might make if it was mashed between two cars. Watery squelch? Bony crunch? Both? A picture flashed in his mind – Hamish doubled over the Barina's bonnet, eyes wide with disbelief, dark blood globbing from his mouth. The image produced a spreading warmth inside Scott's chest, like a shot of gin or the feeling he got when he held his baby son. He remembered a news item he had once seen about a man who had tragically mistaken the accelerator for the brake, and run over his wife.

As Scott's foot hovered between the two pedals he thought of Phil's dedication.

You are not given the desire to do something without the ability to achieve it.

He put his foot down.
Hard.

Saying Goodbye

David Whish-Wilson

There are minutes when I hold it together. When the thoughts don't stray and the clock doesn't leap. But only minutes.

They are hard minutes. The straining of the will to capture the moments. The ember of hope, burning in my gut. Hope that the diagnosis was wrong.

Too real, these minutes. In my darkened bedroom, my sanctuary, where I'm still aware. Where the memories of my wife gather, the clues of her sometime presence: the scarves still hanging off the wardrobe door; her shoes clustered by the drawers; her paperbacks in the bookshelf above our bed.

So real, these minutes. Heightened in every way. But stained, too, by secrets.

The shadows of the flowering marri outside my window – now a sinister projection that shivers on the venetian blind. The sound of the wind beneath the eaves a ghostly voice. The smell of my decrepitude.

I guard these secrets. Incarcerated by my will. But they wish to be free of me. These ghosts.

The only man who stood by me, my favourite snitch. One more soul I have captured. Benny Jones – an alias among many. Christ knows what he heard, what I let slip, when he made his delivery. Off in la-la land. When I returned to myself, the shock of the real bringing tears to my eyes, the powder was there in a neatly folded sheet of paper – *Women's Weekly* I think, lurid colour that burned my eyes – on the bedside table. And a pack of needles. And some plastic bubbles of sterilised water.

I look to the clock, to the page where I wrote the time. It's been hours. I fold myself over the bedside table and begin to work, a pleasing automation in my actions: tip the powder into the saucer, tear and drip the water into the powder, mix the two with the rubber nub of the first needle.

I must have done this many times before. I can feel the ghosts, their pressure, voices bubbling in my throat. The hotshots I've seen. First, Mary Knightshead, in her HJ Holden, parked there by the beach, the sulphur lights of the channel markers winking in the dark. And later, Terry McRae, in his fifteenth-storey bedsit in Johnson Court; watching the sunset over the Indian Ocean, listening to him gurgle, organs haemorrhaging, heart bursting in his chest.

The voices, I can hear them, but I try not to listen. I clamp my mouth shut. But it isn't Mary and Terry that I can hear. It isn't a narration of my life or the sins I've committed. My four children are here. I have invited them. I can hear them, and their spouses, in the kitchen.

I glance at the clock. Four minutes of lucidity. I dare to hope. And I remember, just like last time, how I dared to hope. And I remember, the time before that – perhaps, if I never leave this room, I will get better.

But I write down the time.

Footsteps in the hall. I cap the needles and scoop them into the top drawer, fall back against the pillows. Four pillows. Uncomfortable. My daughter's touch, no doubt.

Why did I invite them?

Of course, to say goodbye.

I can feel my thoughts fizz as the ghosts clamour, as the real becomes unreal, the perimeter between the two as unknowable as the boundary dividing sleep and dream.

I must hold on. So I close my eyes. To hold on.

To listen. Just the one sense to strain – one strand of wire to hold.

My daughter, Sharon. And from the tone of her voice, she's with my youngest son, Greg. Sharon's voice patient, but pitched high – the effect he has on people. My son the meth-head. At thirty-four. Was a junky before that. Somehow lived, when most of his friends died.

Sharon's hand on my shoulder, stroking my brow.

'Ugh,' Greg says. 'How can you do that?'

She doesn't answer. Lifts my left leg onto the bed. At some point it must have slipped off. She holds my dry hand, strokes my wet brow. My only daughter. My beautiful child. Still single. Which I don't mind.

Then they are all here. Through my eyelids I see the orange flare of light. Six people, gathered around. Sharon and the meth-head. Robert and Felicity. Graeme and Ronnie.

What are they doing here?

I wonder if I'm dead. But then Robert, my eldest, says, 'Fucking smell in here.'

Graeme agrees. 'Like he's already dead.'

Sharon doesn't say anything, but she'll be giving them her look, the scathing look delivered across so many dinners, at her brutish brothers.

'What?' Graeme asks.

I was hard on him. It bred nothing but weakness. I like his wife better. She's funnier, smarter, harder. Now she says, 'Sharon's right. Show some respect.'

'Why?' Robert replies. 'It's not like he's compos fucking mentis.'

Sharon sighs. 'There are arrangements we need to make. We have to sell this house to pay for his care. I know it's hard, selling a house full of memories.'

Graeme snorts. 'Memories of what? Him getting stuck in? Shouting at Mum? The big fucking cop hero. Just a thug. A bagman and bash-artist. A driver.'

'Four children and no grandchildren,' Robert says. 'None of us wanted any children. What does that tell you? It tells *me* something.'

'Whatever,' Sharon hisses. 'Greg, what are you doing?'

'Just looking.'

'Greg, no.'

They all chime in, even the boys.

'Leave that stuff alone.'

'It's not yours.'

'It's *ours*.'

'Look, he's crying.' Sharon's hand on my brow again.

'Fucking crocodile tears. Not *even*. Must be automatic.'

'He cried when your mother died.'

'Get out of that, Greg.'

'The fucking smell in here. Let's talk in the kitchen.'

'Greg, for goodness sake…'

And then I am alone.

*

I come back to the world from a place I don't remember. There was no past there and no future, and therefore no present. There was nothing in that place, not even absence; sweet oblivion, a world without ghosts. I look at the clock and where I wrote the time. Three hours have gone.

I remember one thing. I know what Greg was looking for. My guns. Or at least the key to the cabinet in the hall. He will sell them to the goons who keep him supplied, to whom he is surely in debt.

But they're under the house, buried in a toolbox. With the two pineapple grenades and a claymore mine complete with trip wires.

Buried, because I don't trust myself. I have the claymore and grenades for a reason, but that doesn't mean I should keep them on hand, not in my state. I'd kill the postman by accident.

The word is that I'm no longer on the hit-list. Funny that. When my mind was clear, I was a 'dead-man walking', or so I was told, so many times. Now I'm not worth killing. A pitiful old man, haunted and alone – why bother?

But that's just the word on the street. I beat those bastards, the Dingo Jacks, bikie scumbags who'd promised to off me. And they got close. My statesman blown up. A Molotov cocktail put through my bedroom window. A drive-by when I was walking the dog.

I beat those bastards. I survived. On my own.

My own side left me. Officially I'm a dinosaur, a remnant of a wilder time, an embarrassment to the modern force. They spoke of keeping me safe, but their actions spoke louder. They know the secrets I hold, in there with the ghosts in my head. Men who are now at the top of the heap, they learned everything from me. I am not an embarrassment. I am a threat.

And my mind is going. I would talk, but I would not be believed, or even understood. You carry secrets in your gut. I know that because of the ulcers. Buried in the darkness. But it takes will, to keep them there.

My will is gone.

Who am I when I'm absent? A whining fizz? A man who gives it up?

I have seen men make confessions that filled hours of tape. My own would take months. But who will be listening?

They are my shame, those months when I was a dead-man walking. The smell of death in my wake. The old consorter, whose job was to know everyone in the city, every player, every shonk and every hoon. To charm and intimidate, to lubricate the lines of communication. Access for information. I was a powerful man. But after the incident, after the contract was out on me, they all looked on me with pity, or maybe fear. As though the promise of violent death was contagious, liable to spread with a handshake, a nod of the head, a shared drink.

But I endured, and I laughed at them, and I survived. And for what?

Two minutes of lucidity. I hear what my children and their spouses think of me.

What are they doing here?

Of course, I called them home, to say goodbye.

I was no kind of father. A drinker who rarely got drunk. A brawler who rarely got hit. A powerful man, in my own world.

In their world I was less. Distracted, discouraging, given to fits of anger. Not even feared. Merely loathed. Unlike the people I met on the job, my children had no reason to court my favour. Even Sharon, when she was a teenager. Lately she's learned to care. A credit to her mother, who never stopped caring.

Who died when I was a dead-man walking. Her death brought me and Sharon back together. And I have brought Sharon back to tell her about my houses, spread across the city, acquired over decades of careful graft. Even my wife didn't know the extent of my assets. I want Sharon to know.

I write the name of my accountant down, next to his number. Fold the piece of paper, and write Sharon's name.

I hear her defending me, the man she rediscovered after her mother's death. The real me, perhaps. Vulnerable and lonely and desperate, like any man. Charming and funny, too, she told me.

And yet dropped by my friends and enemies alike. The day I stepped over the line, I didn't even know my mind was going. I shot them dead, the four patched members, at their clubhouse. Then I sat in my car for ten minutes. Forgot where I was or what I was doing or had done. Then suddenly I was home, washing my hands in orange juice to remove the gunshot residue.

I got away with it. But I'd crossed the line.

Some lives take a tragic arc. Not my wife, who was loved. Not Sharon, who is successful. And who is loved.

Not my sons, who have never risen above pitiable, despite the brave eyes and fierce words. I have known men just like them. The damaged majority.

And me?

Perhaps.

I was a prince, privy to the ways and the means – the truth behind the charade. Feared when I wasn't admired. Being admired was never enough.

It was the stories and their telling that set me apart, to the select few. In bars and brothels and casinos.

But never secret stories.

Never.

To the grave.

Five minutes of lucidity.

I should write that down.

I hear Sharon defending me. I sense Greg lurking outside the door. The shadows of the marri tree, ghostly on the venetians. The wind in the eaves, a ghostly voice.

My secrets.

'Goodbye,' I croak. Loud enough for Greg to hear, although he does not enter, or return to the others, to tell them that I'm awake.

I sense him there.

'Goodbye,' I say again.

The lamplight, illuminating my old arm as I press home the plunger; the ghosts rising upon me as I fall.

I Hate Crime Fiction

Eddy Burger

I was at my favourite diner, chowing down on a burger with my offsider, Jimmy, when I got a call about a murder. A big-time crime novelist, Miss Tory, had been shot in her hotel room. I polished off my burger in the car as we made for The Grand Incubus, keen to make good time. It was about 10am when I got the call and by 10.15 the hotel was swarming with fans, sticky beaks and the press. Some bellhop had tweeted the whole world before the first cops arrived.

A constable showed us to the victim's body. She was dressed in a nightie and dressing-gown (the victim, not the constable), seated at the desk, slumped over a laptop, exit wound in the back of the head. A funny thing for a crime novelist to be murdered, like she'd been tempting fate or something. Of course, this kind of hubris happened all the time in crime fiction, but in real life it was rare. And this is a true story.

'I bet she ain't wrote about this one,' Jimmy joked.

'But maybe she did, Jimmy,' I said. 'Maybe she did.'

The dame was bent forward like she'd been propped there so the blood could saturate the keyboard. Like the killer was hoping to destroy whatever was on the computer. Had Miss Tory written something the crook was crook about?

Me and Jimmy inspected the scene and got a picture of how it must have gone down. The door to her suite hadn't been forced so we figured the murderer pulled a gun on her when she answered the door. He must have told her his big idea about wanting her to die at her desk, and when she protested, he shot her. Or maybe he was having trouble keeping her quiet so he shut her mouth with a bullet. Then again, maybe it was someone she knew – someone who didn't need a gun to gain admittance. A jilted lover, perhaps, or maybe *he* had jilted *her*. Maybe *she* tried to shoot *him*, but he turned the gun on her by accident. Maybe she had a habit of inviting people to her room just so she could kill them. What a sicko.

It seemed this case was far from open-and-shut, on account of my imagination. I had more imagination in my pinky finger than a dozen crime novelists mulched together in a big concrete blender. But I suppose that's pretty obvious.

Once we were done with the crime scene, we interviewed the neighbouring guests, as well as the bellhop who found the body. I yelled at her (the bellhop, not the body) for tweeting everyone.

'This place is a damn circus!' I said.

'Sorry, Sir. But it's such a crime what happened to Miss Story.'

'What happened to Mystery?'

'It's such a crime!'

'Not necessarily, lass. A mystery could be a thriller, a story of the supernatural or sci-fi. It doesn't have to be crime fiction. I *hate* crime fiction. I don't mean any disrespect to the dead, but the world's hardly any worse off with one less crime writer, is it?'

'Ouch!'

Well, I ditched the conversation then. The kid wasn't making any sense. Neither the bellhop nor the hotel guests had seen or heard anything. I figured the killer must have used a silencer rather than, say, a pillow. There were lots of feathers around Miss Story's suite but we attributed that to her well-known thing for chickens.

The manager showed us recent video surveillance footage. She set us up in a cosy room but we had hardly put our feet up before we spotted the killer – someone dressed as an old man with (blah blah).

[I will omit the less-interesting particulars of this investigation. Readers of crime fiction would no doubt find them riveting but, as I have stated, this is a true story.]

Having thus gained these valuable insights, we then started interviewing (blah blah). We got the staff of the hotel's posh restaurant to assemble in the kitchen. They were a shady-looking bunch. It looked like a police line-up.

'Everyone looks suspicious when you think about it,' said the maître d'. 'During the quieter periods, I occupy myself with sinister thoughts – just a game I play to while away the hours, but you get to wondering about the secret thoughts people are keeping. For example, I might be trying to will someone to stab their husband with a fork, but you'd never think it to look at me. I surprise myself sometimes with the horrors that fill my head, but that's how you have to be when you're a maître d', always polite despite my disgust for the clientele. Take it from me – fancy restaurants are a breeding ground for murderers.'

God, the dame could prattle on. Talk the ears off a brass turd. But I gave her my card and me and Jimmy continued our rounds.

One of the maids said he saw the old man while he was walking along the passage away from the writer's suite.

'There was long auburn hair sticking out from under his wig,' he said. 'But it was definitely a man for I could see stubble on his cheek that wasn't obscured by the fake beard. Judging by the lack of creases around his eyes he must have been under thirty. Oh, and he dropped this hanky.'

The maid shoved the snot rag in my face. 'It has blood on it. I think he had a blood nose.'

'Yeah, I can see that.' I waved it aside. 'Contact me when you find some *real* leads!' Damn amateur detectives!

We went back to the office to study up on Miss Tory and sift through case files. Later that day the girls at forensics got back to us. They'd analysed a strand of hair, a bit of dead skin (blah blah), managed to open the computer's hard drive (blah blah).

'The death of Miss Story's a real mystery, boss,' said Jimmy.

'What the hell are you talking about?'

'The Miss Story mystery.'

'Jesus, Jimmy,' I said. 'Since when did you start stuttering?'

It seemed the case was really getting to him. And he weren't the only one. Cases like this really busted my balls. I was tired of the rigmarole but the tough ones still busted them big-time. Always the same routine: searching for clues, chasing leads (blah blah). I was so bored I started to wish it were me who copped the bullet. But I found consolation in the fact that it was a crime writer who'd copped it.

Such were my feelings at the time – harsh sentiments maybe, and they came back to haunt me soon enough. Another crime novelist was killed, then another and another. Here was a killer who hated cri-fi almost as much as me. At least it cured Jimmy of his stuttering – well, reduced it, anyway. Yet you'd have to do a lot of killing to make a dint in the crime writing industry. Kill a few writers and you only gave the others more to write about. Make mincemeat of the whole industry and there'd be enough material for a dozen new publishing houses. Hundreds even. You'd have to make people afraid not only to write and publish it but to read it as well.

That got me thinking there might be other crimes we could link to the killer – unsolved cases that didn't seem to have a motive, like someone getting shot while reading a book, or for something less serious, like punching a part-time copy editor or perhaps even a florist who just happened to be a closet crime-fiction fan. But there was one hitch: if these crimes were meant to scare, the motive would have to be known. The public would need to know that all these crimes were happening because people actually read that crap.

Me and Jimmy started making a list of likely victims. I rattled off a few from the top of my head: authors, readers, editors, publishers, printers, binders, paper suppliers, ink suppliers, computer manufacturers, book sellers, libraries and librarians, literary agents, publicists, critics and reviewers, book launch venues, book launch caterers, makers of wines, cheeses, crackers, olives and cocktail onions, plus anyone who might have helped or inspired an author, directly or indirectly.

I looked to Jimmy for suggestions. But it seemed like there wasn't much going on upstairs. 'Going too fast for you, am I, Jimmy?'

'No, boss. Me, I was just thinkin' of someone else we could add.'

'Who?'

'You.'

'Me? Phooey! Open your eyes, Jimmy boy. This ain't no fiction. Anyway, who told you you could think?'

We could have thrown around hypotheses all night but it was time we got to studying the unsolved case files. It was a time-consuming business. There was no end to it, particularly since we knew this guy was good at disguises. It made no difference if we had a description of the offender. He could have been African or Chinese, young or old.

'Jesus,' I said to Jimmy. 'This guy could be responsible for every unsolved case in the last ten years!'

'What about this robbery of a convenience store?'

'Ain't you got no imagination? They always stock books. There would have been a few crime books for sure.'

'What about this bike theft?'

'Look where it was stolen from, Jimmy – a train station. The owner probably reads crime novels every time she rides a train.'

'But that ain't the type of crime that's gonna make people afraid of buying books. Who's gonna know?'

'Jesus, Jimmy! That was just a hypothesis. Look at the facts. And who told you you could think?'

Jimmy was getting on my nerves. Sometimes you had to wonder whose side he was on – the side of justice or the side of some lunatic trying to obliterate crime fiction from the face of the earth. Well, *I* was on the lunatic's side on that score, but you can't just go around committing felonies, justifiably or not. It ain't legal.

I took to the streets, leaving Jimmy crashed out on the office sofa. The night was dark and misty with rain but I didn't mind – it was the perfect time for some quiet contemplation. With my trench coat collar turned up I dodged a flooded gutter or two then kicked a tin can for a spell, stopped beneath an awning and lit myself a fag. It was a lonely business, being a dick sometimes. Well, I was a dick all the time... What I mean is that it got lonely sometimes, or would have if not for Jimmy. Walking the streets at night was my only chance to escape.

I quit the awning and wandered aimlessly. Soon I found myself in the vicinity of a familiar window, *her* window – my old flame. The light was on – entertaining guests, no doubt. That dame was trouble with a capital 'T'. She made an hour-glass look pregnant. She had legs up to her armpits and beyond; it would take an entire hosiery factory, working in shifts, to fit them. And she had everyone in town after her. But I had no regrets. We had some fun times. It gave me a warm, fuzzy feeling (in my groin) just thinking about it. Yet now weren't the time for thinking 'bout dames. Not while I was on a case. I doffed my hat and disappeared into the night.

The next day me and Jimmy looked through some *solved* cases, being the last thing our killer would expect. It seemed that *every* crime had been committed by our man, especially when you considered that so many of his victims could have been closet readers. Hundreds of different crimes and hundreds of different felons – thousands, even. There was no way this one guy committed them all, but one thing was certain – I wasn't ruling that out.

I made a list of likely suspects and looked to Jimmy for suggestions but it seemed like there wasn't much going on upstairs.

'Too much for you to take in, hey, Jimmy?'

'No, boss. I was just thinkin' of someone else we could add.'

'Who?'

'You.'

'Me?'

'You hate crime writers so much, maybe you killed Miss Story and the others. Maybe you're behind the whole crime spree!'

'You're kidding! I didn't kill her. I'm the sap spending all his time trying to catch the guy!'

'But maybe that's why we can't find him – because you killed them and you don't want no-one to know.'

'What's your angle, Jimmy? You gonna tell the Chief you think I'm the killer?'

'Oh, no, boss. I wouldn't tell her nothin'. I just thought since we was tryin' to work out who did them killings—'

'You thought it might help me solve the case if I suspected myself.'

'Yeah. That's it, boss. That's what I was thinkin'.'

'Well, keep it to yourself, Jimmy-boy. If anyone else thought the same, it might hamper our investigation somewhat.'

'Sure thing, boss.'

That crazy kid. He had a point, though. I could have been a suspect. Half the force must have heard me mouthing off on how much I hated crime fiction. My motivation would have been the same as the killer's. There were no signs he'd been personally wronged – he just hated that stuff too.

Did I have alibis? Well, some murders had been committed while I was asleep, but people can do strange things when they sleepwalk. I wouldn't hurt a flea when conscious but what about my unconscious? Was it capable of murder? Well, I wasn't asleep during *all* the murders, but perhaps there was more than one killer. In any case, it was high time I saw a hypnotherapist and got to the bottom of it. Cases like this really busted my balls.

But before I had a chance to make the appointment we got our first big break. We'd been going through case files late one night when Jimmy popped out for a soft drink; when he came back he threw me a letter.

'Must have been delivered late,' he said. 'Might be important.'

It had my name on the envelope, spelt with letters cut out of newspapers. The note inside was likewise.

I am the killer of crime novelists. It may interest you to know that among the many other crimes I have committed, I was recently convicted for indecent exposure at a book signing.

'Jesus,' I said. 'It must have taken ages to cut out and stick down all them letters. He'd have to be unemployed or casually employed or else he'd never find the time – unless he shirks on other things, like doing laundry. My guess is that he works in a job where it don't matter how much he stinks, like cleaning stables or selling real estate.'

Meanwhile, Jimmy was fiddling with the envelope.

'*Get your head out of the clouds, Jimmy,*' I barked. 'You've got to be on the ball if you want to get anywhere in this game!'

'But boss. The killer put his name on the back of the envelope.'

He handed it to me and there was the sender's name, sure enough, written with the same cut-out lettering – Mr Iyhait Krymphixshon. It was surrounded with arrows pointing to it. 'A queer name but it sounds legit,' I said. 'Who'd make up a name like *Iyhait Krymphixshon?*'

I searched the files and sure enough he'd been convicted of half-a-dozen misdemeanours over the last few months, including the flashing incident. The reports said he had appeared increasingly agitated at each hearing and he always made a big issue of the wig and fake beard he wore. 'I wear the same wig and beard for every crime I commit!' he stated. There were photos of the wig and beard among the various photographed items of evidence, as well as photos of him wearing them.

'Hold on to your hat, Jimmy,' I said. 'I think I'm onto something.'

'But I'm not wearing a hat, boss.'

'Shut up and watch! You might learn a thing or two.'

I remembered that the killer had (blah blah). Then I played the tape and there it was! He was wearing the very same wig and beard!

'Thought he could pull the wool over my eyes, hey,' I said. 'Well, he ain't so smart. He ain't so smart at all.'

'But it looks to me like he wanted to be caught,' said Jimmy.

'Rubbish! I think it's time we paid Mr Krymphixshon a visit.'

'What if it's a trap?'

'A trap? If anything's a trap, it's me. I'm the trap. Anyway, who told you you could think?'

'But maybe there's other hypotheses.'

'Rubbish!'

'What about the letter, and the wig and beard – how he's making such a big deal—'

Jimmy collapsed in his chair. I had chloroformed him. It was a last resort, you understand. He couldn't see sense if it was stapled to his eyeballs – though having your eyeballs stapled mightn't help you see much. Anyway, he was hampering the investigation. We had to act now – nab the killer before he realised his mistake and skipped town. It was late – after midnight – but as good a time as any. I made ready to leave. Yet the question of whether it was a trap still dogged me. Jimmy's reasoning had made no sense, but if there was even the slightest chance, I had to be prepared. Normally, if we was making a bust on a serial killer, we'd bring half the force, but that might have been just what this killer wanted. On the other hand, if he knew we'd be thinking that, or if he knew that we knew that he knew, well, there was no telling what the fuck could happen. The bottom line was I couldn't risk losing good cops. Call me a hero or call me daft, I was going to face this demon alone.

I carried Jimmy out to the car and threw him in the boot. Well, I couldn't just leave him drooling on the office furniture, but I weren't keen on him waking up neither, so the two of us headed off for the killer's (blah blah), a warehouse in the industrial (blah blah). I crept down the passage, pausing at every turn, bracing myself at every open door, listening for the slightest sound. The place seemed deserted but it was hard to tell in the darkness. I had a torch, but I didn't switch it on in case it attracted too much attention. Then I fell down some stairs, though I couldn't see them, just feel them. They were metal and made an awful racket. I would have woken the dead if they hadn't already been woken by the racket I made when I busted into the place.

At the bottom of the stairs, I shakily got to my feet. But suddenly I noticed, right in front of me, a monster of a man! He had the most frightful, sinister appearance. Then I realised he was holding a torch close to his chin, purposefully angled to make him appear scary. How immature can you get? How pathetic. I had to laugh. I laughed and laughed – and that's when I realised it was myself I was seeing in a mirror.

Instinctively, I shone the torch around to see if anyone had witnessed my performance. The torch light fell on a wall covered with photos, newspaper clippings and scribbled notes, connected by bits of string crisscrossing everywhere. Just about everything was connected to a photo of me!

I took a step closer and bumped a table, shone my torch on it and realised someone was seated there. He wore a pair of night-vision goggles and gazed right at me. Before I could turn my gun on him, he pressed a barrel to my head.

'Drop it, you sorry excuse for a detective.'

I placed my gun gently on the table.

'God, you really are stupid,' he said.

'Who are you calling stupid, chauvinist!'

'I don't think you're stupid just because you're a woman! God! I'm a woman too!'

'You mean ... we're *both* women?'

'Yes!'

'What about the stubble the maid saw?'

'Jesus, you're even dumber than you look! I'm amazed they put you on my case. Perhaps the chief of police hates crime fiction too.'

'I wouldn't get so cocky if I was you, Krymphixshon. Any second now the—'

'My name's *Iyhait* Krymphixshon! Never leave off the Iyhait!'

'Come on. It's always the surname used by authorities and the press – *the Krymphixshon case, Krymphixshon versus the state*—'

'You bet it is!'

'What?'

'It's trying to take over the state! It's a scourge on our society – a threat to the integrity of the human race!'

'Crime fiction?'

'I told you not to call me that!'

'What the hell are you talking about?'

'Crime fiction. Fictional detectives are the worst – hard-nosed sleuths as individualistic as ants. But still crime writers churn them out, the same characters, same scenarios, same framework, over and over.'

'What are you telling me for? I ain't no fictional detective.'

'Of course you are.'

'Bullshit. I'm the real deal. I hate crime fiction.'

'What?'

I Hate Crime Fiction

'What do you mean *what*?'

'You just said Iyhait Krymphixhon.'

'What the hell are you talking about?'

'You *are* a fictional detective. Your story is being written right now, as we speak.'

'You're mad!'

'Oh, I'm not the mad one. I knew he'd have to bring us face to face eventually.'

'Who?'

'The writer of this story! The source! He thinks he's so clever, writing a crime story that's anti-crime fiction, with all this postmodern authorial-intrusion crap. But he's not anti-crime fiction. He's perpetuating it, just like the rest of them! Or worse – laying the foundations for a new take on the genre!'

'What the hell are you talking about? I'm not doing any of that crap!'

'I'm not talking to you! I'm addressing the author.'

'The author?'

'The gig is up, Burger!'

'What the hell do Burgers have to do with anything?'

'Burger is the author's name! Now shut up!'

'Burger? You're kidding me.'

'It's you I aim to kill!' said Krymphixshon to the author. 'Now raise your hands from the keyboard!'

The End

Ending 2

'You can't refer to the writer's keyboard!' said Jimmy. 'You're distancing the reader!'

'Jimmy!' I said. 'I'm glad to see you. Krymphixshon has lost her marbles.'

'I told you not to call me Krymphixshon!' yelled Krymphixshon.

Jimmy had his gun on Krymphixshon but then he trained it on me.

'What are the hell are you doing, Jimmy? Are you nuts?'

'No way, boss. If this writer really is controlling everything, then he's the one responsible for the murders. Since this is a first-person narrative, you practically *are* the writer.'

'That's crazy talk, Jimmy! Put the gun down!'

'It ain't crazy! You're always havin' a dig at me, talkin' to me like I'm retarded or somethin'!'

'Oh, I see. This isn't about the murders at all, is it? Anyway, who told you you could think?'

(blah blah)

'There's no way you can kill the writer!' yelled Jimmy to Krymphixshon. 'He's writing everything you do!'

'I got this far, didn't I! Maybe he wants to be shot.'

'But what are you gonna shoot at? You can't see him. He's nowhere and everywhere – omnipresent, like a god.'

'I could give him a heart attack. He could get too close to his creations, lose sight of reality and then have a heart attack from the horror of it all.'

Jimmy cried, 'How do you know you won't just kill a reader?'

'A reader? But it hasn't been published yet!'

'I think it has.'

'Nonsense!'

'This story will end when one of the main characters gets killed.'

'Then kill Krymphixshon!' I yelled. 'For god's sake!'

Suddenly Krymphixshon shot Jimmy in the chest. He went down like he was winched to the floor. I checked his pulse but there weren't none. I pulled open his shirt – Jimmy had breasts! Jimmy was a dame, too! The bullet had gone straight through her heart.

I reached across the floor for Jimmy's gun but Krymphixshon had her barrel to my head faster than if it had been glued there all along.

'I wouldn't touch that gun if I were you,' she said. 'Besides, if what your friend Jimmy said is true, it would be better for you if neither of us died. We're the main characters.'

'I don't need to kill you to see justice done. They'll lock you away for life!'

'You can't arrest me. If you do, the case will be closed and the story will end.'

'Do you expect me to let you just walk away, scot-free?'

'Don't forget who's holding the gun. I could shoot you anytime.'

'I suppose you're right.'

'And don't think you can beguile me with your feminine whiles, temptress!'

'What the hell are you talking about? I was only adjusting my bra! God!'

'I think it's time for you to leave.'

With her gun to my back, Krymphixshon showed me out the door.

I called for backup the moment I was outside but by the time they arrived Krymphixshon had flown the coop. They carried Jimmy's body away. I had mixed feelings about my old sidekick, but I would never have wished her dead. There was a lot of explaining to do back at (blah blah). Cases like this really busted my ovaries.

It had been a long night. With a couple of hours left before sunrise, I took to the streets and lost myself in the rain, paused beneath an awning, lit myself a fag and I thought about that strange conversation between Jimmy and Krymphixshon. Surely it was bonkers to think this was all part of a story by some writer. My life wouldn't end if Krymphixshon died or went to prison. Besides, my job was done. We knew who the murderer was and it was just a matter of time before she was nabbed. My story could hardly go on if I never saw her again. It might as well end right now.

The End

Ending 3

After more wandering, I found myself once again prowling the neighbourhood of my old flame. Her bedroom light was on. I felt game enough to give her another shot. The worst she could do was shut the door in my face, and that was nothing compared to the wringer I'd been through lately. I picked up a pebble and threw it at her window. In a moment she opened it and looked down angrily, but her expression changed the moment she saw it was me.

'Oh, Edwina! Edwina!' she cried joyously. 'I thought you'd given up on me!'

'Can I come in for a nightcap?'

She vanished from the window and reappeared before me in the doorway. My old flame, every bit as ravishing as the day we'd met. If this was a dream, you could shoot me now, I thought. It would be better than shooting me if this wasn't a dream because then I would die.

She held out her hand to me and led me inside. What was to follow was beyond words … but that's another story.

The End

CRIME SCENES

Contributors

TONY BIRCH's books include *Shadowboxing* (Scribe, 2006), *Father's Day* (Hunter, 2009), *Blood* (UQP, 2011), *The Promise* (UQP, 2014) and *Ghost River* (UQP, 2015). He is currently a Research Fellow in the Moondani Balluk Academic Unit at Victoria University.

CARMEL BIRD is the author of thirty books, the most recent being a short story collection, *My Hearts Are Your Hearts* (Spineless Wonders, 2015), and an extended essay, *Fair Game* (Finlay Lloyd, 2015). Her *Dear Writer Revisited* and *Writing the Story of Your Life* are widely used by students of writing. carmelbird.com | carmel-bird.blogspot.com

EDDY BURGER is a Melbourne writer of funny and experimental fiction and poetry. His work has appeared in Australian and international journals and anthologies. He has had chapbooks published by the Melbourne Poets Union and Small Change Press. Eddy is an anti-realist, postmodernist and champion of the imagination. He was runner-up in the 2015 Carmel Bird Award for New Crime Writing.

PETER CORRIS has been a full-time writer since the early 1980s. He has published more than 70 works of fiction and about a dozen non-fiction titles. He is best known for his series about Sydney private detective Cliff Hardy. The 41st book in the series, *That Empty Feeling*, was published in 2016.

MELANIE NAPTHINE is a Melbourne-based writer. She has recently won the Boroondara, Ethel Webb Bundell and Margaret River Short Story competitions and was shortlisted in the Overland, Katharine Susannah Pritchard, Olga Masters and Henry Handel Richardson competitions and was runner-up in the 2015 Carmel Bird Award for New Crime Writing. She works in educational publishing, and any time left over is spent reading, running, travelling and parenting.

ANDREW NETTE is a Melbourne-based writer and journalist. He is the author of two novels, *Ghost Money* (Crime Waves Press, 2012), a crime story set in mid-nineties Cambodia, and *Gunshine State* to be published by 280 Steps in 2016. His short fiction has appeared in a number of print and online publications. His online home is pulpcurry.com | @Pulpcurry

After 13 years in the NSW Police **PM NEWTON** went to Mali to write about music and India to study Buddhist philosophy. Award-winning author of *The Old School* (2011) and *Beams Falling (2011) published* by Penguin Books Australia. *H*er short fiction and essays have appeared in *The Intervention Anthology (2015)*, *The Great Unknown* (Spineless Wonders, 2013), *Seizure*, *Review of Australian Fiction* and *Anne Summers Reports*. 'The Mango Tree' first appeared in *Making Tracks: UTS Writers' Anthology*. pmnewton.com

AMANDA O'CALLAGHAN's short stories and flash fiction have been published and won awards in Australia, UK and Ireland. Amanda won the 2015 Carmel Bird Award for New Crime Writing. A former advertising executive, she has an MA in English from King's College, London. She holds a PhD in English from the University of Queensland. Amanda lives in Brisbane.

LEIGH REDHEAD has worked on a prawn trawler and as a waitress, exotic dancer, masseuse, teacher and apprentice chef. She is the author of the award-winning Simone Kirsch private eye series: *Peepshow* (2004), *Rubdown* (2005) *Cherry Pie* (2007) and *Thrill City* (2010), published by Allen & Unwin. She is currently completing the fifth in the series while studying for a PhD in Australian noir fiction.

ANGELA SAVAGE is an award-winning Melbourne writer, who has lived and travelled extensively in Asia. Her Jayne Keeney PI series, including *Behind the Night Bazaar* (2006), *The Half-Child* (2010) and *The Dying Beach* (2013), is set in Thailand and published by Text Publishing. She won the 2011 Scarlett Stiletto Award for her short story 'The Teardrop Tattoos'. Angela is studying for her PhD in Creative Writing.

angelasavage.wordpress.com | @angsavage

Winner of the Ernest Hemingway Flash Fiction Award, **MICHAEL CALEB TASKER** was born in Montreal, Canada and spent his childhood New Orleans. He has been published in numerous literary journals including *Shenandoah, Ellery Queen's Mystery Magazine, The New Ohio Review*. He was runner-up in the 2014 John Steinbeck Short Fiction Contest and in the 2015 Carmel Bird Award for New Crime Writing.

DAVID WHISH-WILSON is the author of two crime novels set in 1970s Perth – *Line of Sight* (2010) and *Zero at the Bone* (2013) published by Penguin Books Australia. His most recent publication is the *Perth* book in the NewSouth Books city series. The third novel in the Frank Swann series – *Old Scores* – is due for release in 2016. David lives in Fremantle, Western Australia, where he coordinates the creative writing program at Curtin University.

Editor

ZANE LOVITT's story 'Leaving the Fountainhead' won the SD Harvey Short Story Award at the 2010 Ned Kelly Awards for Australian crime fiction, while his debut novel, *The Midnight Promise*, won the 2013 Ned Kelly Award for Best First Fiction. That same year he was named a *Sydney Morning Herald* Best Young Australian Novelist. His second novel, *Black Teeth*, will be available in July, 2016 through Text Publishing.

Spineless Wonders publications are available in print and digital format from participating bookshops and online. For further information about where to purchase our print and ebooks, go to the Spineless Wonders website:

www.shortaustralianstories.com.au

Printed in Australia
AUOC02n0807290416
275563AU00002B/2/P

9 781925 052237